R

Jon Athan

For more information on this book or the
author, please visit www.jon-athan.com. General
inquiries are welcome.

Facebook:
https://www.facebook.com/AuthorJonAthan
Twitter: @Jonny_Athan
Email: info@jon-athan.com

Book cover by Paramita:
http://www.creativeparamita.com/

Thank you for the support!

ISBN-13: 978-1976321795
ISBN-10: 1976321794

First Edition

WARNING

This book contains scenes of intense violence and some disturbing themes. Some parts of this book may be considered violent, cruel, disturbing, or unusual. Certain implications may also trigger strong emotional responses. This book is *not* intended for those easily offended or appalled. Please enjoy at your own discretion.

Table of Contents

Chapter One..1
Chapter Two..13
Chapter Three..23
Chapter Four..29
Chapter Five...37
Chapter Six...51
Chapter Seven...57
Chapter Eight...67
Chapter Nine...87
Chapter Ten...97
Chapter Eleven...109
Chapter Twelve..117
Chapter Thirteen..123
Chapter Fourteen...137
Chapter Fifteen...149
Chapter Sixteen..157
Chapter Seventeen...167
Chapter Eighteen..179
Chapter Nineteen...187

Chapter One

Happy Birthday

"Have you ever thought about killing someone?" Kevin White asked, leaning back on his tattered computer chair.

At seventeen years old, Kevin was a reclusive high school student. He always wore black from head-to-toe—faded t-shirts, tight jeans, and shabby sneakers. His black hair was buzz cut, short and neat. Deviance glimmered in his zany blue eyes. He was a recluse, but he wasn't anxious or shy. He was just different—and *different* wasn't often welcomed by teenagers.

The young man smirked as he stared at his thirteen-year-old brother, Jacob White. He was amused by the look of awe on his face. He thought: *he's just like me, isn't he?*

Jacob sat on Kevin's bed, directly across from his older sibling. He stared at his brother with a set of narrowed eyes and an open mouth. The question was short and simple, but he couldn't understand it. He never thought he would hear such a strange question from someone as young as his brother. As far as he knew, murder wasn't a popular subject among teenagers.

Jacob wasn't like his brother. He had feathery black hair, which covered his forehead. His blue eyes were dull and listless. Fashion wasn't important to him, so he wore whatever he could find. In the dingy bedroom, he wore a blue windbreaker jacket over a button-up shirt, blue jeans, and sneakers. However, *like* his brother, he was a recluse who liked to blend with the crowds.

He sucked his lips inward and stared down at himself. He didn't know how to answer his brother's question.

Kevin knocked on his computer desk and asked, "Well, have you or haven't you?"

"Why are you asking me that, Kev?"

"That doesn't matter right now, does it? Just answer the question."

Jacob shook his head and said, "No, man. I've never thought about it before."

"Interesting..."

Kevin glanced around his puny bedroom. Posters of horror movies and video games clung to the charcoal-colored walls. The floorboards creaked and groaned with the slightest movement. A slit of sunshine poured through the closed curtains on the window over his bed. The pungent stench of dirty laundry stained the room, too. To a careless recluse like Kevin, the room was cozy.

Kevin said, "You know, I've been waiting a long time for this day. Years, actually."

Jacob furrowed his brow and asked, "What? Why? It's just my birthday. I have a birthday every year and it's always the same thing. What's so special about this year?"

"You're thirteen now, Jacob. Usually, people think they're adults when they turn eighteen or twenty-one. When they buy cigarettes or beer, they think they're grown. That's not true, though. No, little man, *I* think you become an adult when you're thirteen. I mean, *I've* been acting like an adult since the day I turned thirteen. I don't drink or smoke or do shit like that, but I've been doing... adult 'things' for a while now. Anyway, since you're thirteen today, I want to have a *very* serious talk with you later."

"We're talking now, aren't we?"

Kevin nodded and said, "Yeah, you're right. We can't talk about it right now, though. There are too many people here today—too many eyes, too many ears. Come back to my room around midnight. I'm going to show you a secret. It's going to change your world, little man."

Jacob tilted his head and swallowed loudly, blatantly nervous. His gulp could be heard from the hallway. *Secret*—the word echoed through his mind. A secret could be anything, but he figured it had something to do with murder. *Why else would he ask me about killing people?*–he thought.

Jacob asked, "What's the secret?" Kevin smiled, crossed his arms, and shook his head—*I'm not telling you now.* Jacob said, "Come on. At least give me a hint. Is... Is it something I can see? Or is it something about you? Does it... Does it have something to do with your question? Seriously, what is it?"

Kevin responded, "Just come back to my room tonight. Don't worry, I think you're going to like it."

Knocking emerged from the bedroom door behind Kevin. The knob turned, then the hinges squealed as the door swung open. The brothers glanced over at the door.

Isabel White, their forty-year-old mother, stood in the doorway. Her short wispy hair reached down to the nape of her neck. Her face appeared chiseled thanks to her lean figure. She wore a low-cut tank top, exposing her large cleavage. Her jeans were tight, too, showcasing her other curves. To be blunt, the woman was a certified MILF.

Isabel asked, "What are you boys doing in here?"

"We're just talking," Kevin responded. He turned towards Jacob and said, "I wanted to wish my brother a happy birthday before everyone else. Family first, you know?"

"That's sweet and all, but I need the both of you to come out to the backyard to join the party. We can't have a birthday party without the birthday boy. That's just not how it works. Come on."

Jacob said, "Okay, I'll be out in a minute."

"Okay. Well, we'll be waiting for you."

Isabel closed the door. The sound of her high heels *thudding* on the creaky floorboards seeped into the bedroom.

Kevin shook his head and whispered, "Nice tits, mom. Who are you trying to sink your teeth into this time?"

Jacob raised his brow, surprised by his brother's crass words. He never heard his brother talk about their mother's breasts before. It was jarring and awkward.

Upon spotting Jacob's baffled expression, Kevin explained, "Don't act like you don't know, Jacob.

She's only wearing *that* because she's trying to fuck some guy."

Jacob shrugged and stuttered, "O–Okay..."

"I'm serious. Just take a look at her when you're out there. She's going to be all over the young guys. I guarantee it."

Kevin stood from his seat. He stared down at his younger brother and nodded, communicating without uttering a word—*see you soon.* Jacob reluctantly returned the nod. He didn't know anything about his brother's secret, but he trusted him. The brothers exited the room and headed to the backyard.

***

Parents and children from the neighborhood gathered in the backyard for a barbecue. Some adults stood near the grill, drinking and bantering as they cooked burgers and hot dogs. The older parents found shelter under the large patio umbrellas at the tables, despite the overcast sky. The children ran on the grass, slipping and sliding as they sprayed each other with water guns.

Jacob stood near a large tree at the farthest end of the backyard. He watched his peers with downcast eyes. To his dismay, he wasn't invited to play. The truth was difficult to admit, especially for a teenager, but he couldn't deny it: *he was a loner.* He didn't have any real friends. His mother invited the parents of his classmates, so the kids were dragged to his party.

He frowned and shook his head, flustered. Envy was an odd emotion. The innocent happiness of one person could cause sorrow to another person. Every smile appeared smug and arrogant while laughter sounded like nails on a chalkboard. Yet, envy dominated the boy's mind—tormenting him. He thought: *why can't I be like them? Why don't they like me?*

Jacob glanced over at his small tumbledown house, then he stared at the overgrown grass in the backyard. He lived in a lower-class neighborhood, but he always felt like the poorest child in the entire city. He was ashamed of his poverty. Poverty wasn't synonymous with popularity after all.

"Happy birthday, faggot," a nasally male voice said from Jacob's right.

Jacob glanced over at the source of the voice. He already knew who was calling out to him, the voice had haunted him since elementary school, but he still hoped a long-lost friend would approach. *Faggot*—the slur wasn't exactly friendly, though. So, the frown remained on his face.

Wyatt Anderson, his personal bully, approached the tree. The red-haired, roly-poly teenager—round but strong—was accompanied by two lanky teenagers. The lanky teenagers always followed Wyatt, acting like an entourage of bullies. The group stopped in front of Jacob.

In a sarcastic tone, Wyatt said, "Thanks for inviting my mom to your party, Jacob. I really like *wasting* my time at your poor-ass house."

Keeping his head down, Jacob responded, "I didn't ask her to invite you."

"Don't lie to me, punk. Your mom invited

everyone in the whole damn city. She's probably looking for some cock to gobble up."

Eric, one of the lanky teenagers, said, "You should ask her if she wants yours, Wyatt."

"Yeah, man. You can be this faggot's dad," David, the other slender bully, said.

Wyatt chuckled, then he said, "I might, I might. Shit, man, did you see what she was wearing? Look at those tits, man. I would fuck the shit out of her."

"Fuck you," Jacob muttered.

Wyatt furrowed his brow and asked, "What did you just say?"

"N–Nothing. I was–"

Mid-sentence, Wyatt shoved Jacob to the ground. Surprised, Jacob crawled in reverse until his back hit the tree.

Wyatt said, "Watch your fuckin' mouth, you little bitch."

Jacob glanced over at the adults standing near the grill. Unfortunately, the parents were so engrossed with their gossip that they didn't notice the bullying occurring only ten meters away.

Wyatt stepped in front of Jacob's view and said, "Listen to me, punk. When this is all over, you're going to give us all of the money and gifts you get. I know my mom is giving you twenty dollars in a stupid-ass birthday card today. You better bring me my money tomorrow or else."

Jacob remained quiet. Although he endured years of bullying, he still didn't know how to deal with Wyatt. He could always appease him, but he knew that wouldn't stop a bully. He could run, but he wouldn't get far. He could scream, but that would only fluster his bully. He was pushed to a corner.

Wyatt chuckled as he examined Jacob's frightened demeanor. *Pussy,* he thought, *I could make him piss his pants right now.*

He pulled a switchblade out of his pocket. With a press of a button, a three-inch blade protruded from the handle. He held the knife in front of his stomach so the adults wouldn't see it.

Jacob's eyes widened with fear as he stared at the blade. He shuddered and stammered, but he couldn't scream or run. His fear paralyzed him.

Wyatt whispered, "I could shank you right now. What do you think of that, huh? I could make you squeal like a pig."

"Are you boys okay over there?" a man in a turtleneck sweater asked, casually flipping a patty on the grill.

Wyatt pressed the button again and retracted the blade. He dropped the switchblade on the ground, then he kicked it deeper into the overgrown grass.

With a smile plastered on his face, he glanced back at the adults and shouted, "We're okay! Jacob just tripped on a rock. You know how he is!"

The concerned man smiled and waved at them—*okay.* He continued grilling, blissfully unaware of the violent bullying.

Wyatt said, "Come on, let's get out of here before we get busted. I'll come get the knife later. I have more at home anyway." As they walked away, Wyatt muttered, "We'll get that faggot at school. Fuck him."

Jacob closed his eyes and sighed in relief. The

bullying would continue later, but the episode ended on a decent note. *No broken bones, no cuts, no bruises,* he thought, *so far, so good.* A day without being stabbed was a good day.

"Hi, Jacob," a girl's voice said.

Jacob opened his eyes and glanced at his right. Molly Moore, a blonde-haired classmate, approached. She sat next to him. She smiled as she scooted closer to him, then she leaned back on the tree. Jacob smiled and blushed. He liked Molly, but he couldn't admit it. She was his first real crush after all.

Molly asked, "Are you liking your party?"

Jacob shrugged and responded, "It's okay, I guess. I mean, it looks like everyone is having fun."

"Are *you* having fun?"

"Um... I don't know. I never really liked parties. There's too many people. It makes me... uncomfortable."

"Yeah, I know what you mean. I don't like big crowds, either. I guess we're just shy."

Jacob glanced over at Molly, his eyes glittering with hope. He appreciated her understanding attitude.

As she stared at the adults, Molly said, "I saw Wyatt pushing you earlier. He's such a jerk. I'm sorry about that... Are you okay?"

"I–I'm... I'm fine. He pushed me, but I *really* tripped on a rock. He... He's not that strong."

"He just acts that way 'cause he's bigger than everyone else. If you want, I can tell on him for you. He can't call you a snitch if I do it, right?"

The offer was kind and sincere, but it was also ignorant and foolish. Bullies didn't care about semantics. The victim of a bully would always endure the consequences of another person's actions—and the bully would never have to justify his bullying. The victim acted as a sponge, soaking up the bully's rage.

Jacob said, "Thanks, but... I'm okay. Like I said, I just fell over. Don't worry about it."

Molly nodded and said, "Okay. Just let me know if you ever want me to help." She glanced over at the tables and grill. She said, "I wonder what kind of gifts everyone got you. I think they're mostly birthday cards. Maybe some–"

Molly's words became a stream of indecipherable nonsense, muffled and distorted. Jacob's attention was captured by his mother.

Isabel stood next to a young man near the grill, her hand on his bicep and her breasts pressed up against his shoulder. She whispered into his ear, then she simpered—*mischievous*. She clearly flirted with him. The man appeared to be in his early twenties. He wasn't a parent or an older brother of anyone in Jacob's class. He was a new member of the neighborhood. Judging from his limited interactions with the kids at the party, he didn't seem interested in children.

Isabel couldn't keep her hands off of him, though. She wasn't looking for a father for her children, she was simply looking for sex.

Jacob was embarrassed by his mother's lascivious behavior. He could see Wyatt and his friends staring at her, snickering as they leered at her cleavage. Some of the adults even glanced over at her, amused by her behavior.

Jacob spotted his older brother sitting at the end of one of the tables, eating a hamburger by his lonesome. Kevin smirked and shrugged at Jacob, as if to say: *I told you so.* Jacob responded with a nod— *you were right.*

"Jacob!" Isabel shouted from the grill, stretching her neck to look over the crowd. She smiled upon spotting her son near the tree. She beckoned to him and yelled, "Come on, sweetie! It's time to cut the cake!"

Jacob sighed in disappointment. He staggered to his feet and brushed the dirt off his jeans. He nervously smiled as he helped Molly stand up. All of the children gathered around one of the patio tables, eager to get a slice of the cake.

Jacob shambled towards his mother near the center of the table. Isabel placed her hands on his shoulders and pulled him in front of her.

Isabel said, "Okay. Are you all ready to sing? One, two, three..."

The kids and adults performed a discordant rendition of the classic *Happy Birthday* song. Their dull voices overlapped as they forced themselves through the song. Frankly, no one cared about Jacob's birthday. The kids were there for cakes and games, the adults were there for free food and gossip.

As the song ended, Isabel nudged Jacob forward and said, "Go ahead, sweetie. Make a wish and blow out the candles."

Jacob closed his eyes and took a deep breath. He didn't believe in the tradition, his wishes never came true, but he figured it wouldn't hurt. He thought: *I wish I could be like everyone else, I wish everyone liked me.* He opened his eyes and blew out the candles.

As the adults clapped, Wyatt grabbed the back of Jacob's head, then he thrust Jacob's face into the cake. The bully shouted, "Happy birthday, man! How does it taste?"

"Wyatt! What do you think you're doing?" a woman snapped at him.

Jacob couldn't see the woman on account of the chocolate frosting covering his eyes. He safely assumed the shrill voice belonged to Wyatt's mother, though. He also assumed the woman would scold Wyatt for his bad behavior, but Wyatt would remain the same. He could hear the other parents dismissing Wyatt's behavior as 'boy stuff.'

As he wiped the cake from his eyes, Jacob glanced over at his brother. He caught a glimpse of the malicious glimmer in Kevin's eyes. He wasn't glaring at Jacob, though. Kevin's livid eyes were locked on Wyatt. *What are you thinking, Kev? What are you planning?*–Jacob thought.

Chapter Two

That Night

Jacob lay in bed and stared at the ceiling, anxiously waiting for the clock to strike midnight. He squirmed and groaned in bed—nervous, excited, *embarrassed.* Through the house's thin walls, he could hear a rhythmic *thumping* sound. His mother's gentle moans and a man's aggressive grunts accompanied the thumping.

The fact couldn't be denied: the young man from the party was fucking his mother. As a matter of fact, they had been having sex for the past two hours.

Jacob knew it was the man from the party because he had already seen him walk past his bedroom to get a drink from the kitchen during their intermissions. Then, the man would return to the master bedroom to fuck Isabel again. The relationship was simple: sex and *only* sex.

Jacob wrapped his pillow around his head and groaned. He thought about the bullies and their insults. He thought about his mother and her lustful actions. One question echoed through his young, impressionable mind: *is my mom a slut?* He didn't have an answer. He glanced over at the clock and sighed in relief. The clock read: *12:03.*

He whispered, "Finally."

With his shoulders and heels raised, he crept out

of his bedroom. He stopped in the hallway, grimacing in disgust. His mother's moans were louder than before, drilling into his ears. There were two doors on the other side of the hall. The door to the right led to the master bedroom, the door to the left led to Kevin's room.

Jacob opened his brother's door. He stood in the doorway and stared into the gloomy bedroom. The room was solely illuminated by the light from the computer monitor on the left side of the room. A pornographic video of a Japanese woman being molested on a train played on the monitor. Of course, it was censored and fake. The bedroom appeared to be empty, though.

Jacob coughed to clear his throat, then he said, "I'm here."

A *thud* emerged from the closet on the right side of the room, as if someone had fallen over and clashed with the wall. The thudding sounds continued for ten seconds, then the closet door swung open.

Kevin emerged from the closet, lifting his pajama bottoms up to his waist. He was shirtless, so Jacob could see the sweat glistening on his lean figure.

Jacob asked, "What were you doing in there?"

Kevin smirked and said, "It's a secret."

"A secret? Is that what you wanted to talk to me about?"

As he sat on his bed, Kevin said, "Nope. I'll tell you about the closet later. You're not ready for it." He beckoned to Jacob and said, "Sit down next to me. Don't be shy, little man. I'm not going to hurt you."

Jacob sighed and stared down at himself. He counted the thin stripes on his flannel pajamas. He didn't have a reason to distrust his brother. Yet, he still found himself doubting Kevin's intentions. He thought: *what do you want from me, Kev?* He closed the door behind him, then he shambled towards the bed.

Without making eye contact, he sat on the bed beside his brother. The siblings sat in the gloomy room, quiet and anxious. Only the sound of their mother's sex—a lustful symphony of natural music —seeped into the bedroom. Kevin already came to terms with the noise since he had been hearing it for years. Jacob still thought it was awkward.

As he stared at his brother, Kevin asked, "Jacob, would you tell on me if I told you I did 'bad' things?"

Jacob stared down at his lap and twiddled his thumbs as he thought about the question. *Bad things*—the words could mean anything to different people. It was *bad* to curse around elders, it was *bad* to ditch school, and it was *bad* to hurt people. *What's the worst a teenager could do?*

Jacob shrugged and said, "Well, you never told on me for anything, so I guess I wouldn't tell on you."

Kevin responded, "That's good. It's... It's *honorable*. Yeah, I think that's the right word." He took a deep breath as he glanced around the room, as if he were reminiscing about the past. He said, "I don't think I'm doing 'bad' things. But, if other people found out about what I was doing, they'd probably think I was *very* bad. So, this has to be kept a secret. You can't tell anyone about this, okay? If you do, they're going to send me away for good. You understand me?"

Jacob stared at his brother with narrowed eyes—horrified but curious. His brother stared back at him with a steady facial expression. The conversation was serious.

Jacob stuttered, "I–I don't... I don't know about this, Kev. Maybe... Maybe you should just keep it to yourself."

"I can't. It's hard to explain, but I... I have to tell someone. It's eating me alive. Besides, we're family. I see a little bit of myself in you. I think you'll like my secret. I have a good feeling about this. Will you keep my secret? *Please?*"

Jacob could feel the sincerity in his brother's voice. He sighed and nodded in agreement, as if to say: *fine, I'll keep your secret.* Kevin grinned from ear-to-ear, pleased by his brother's response. He rushed over to his bedroom door and turned the lock, then he sat on his computer chair. Yet again, the brothers sat in silence.

Kevin smiled and stared down at the floor as he thought about his confession. His words had to be precise in order to keep his brother's trust. Jacob simply watched his brother, anxiously waiting for the revelation. The possibilities ran through his mind, but he couldn't focus due to his mother's incessant moaning.

Kevin said, "Okay, alright... This might be hard to believe, but it's true—*100-percent true.* Believe me, Jacob, I wouldn't lie to you." He nervously chuckled, struggling to keep his composure. He said, "Like I told you earlier, I became a man when I turned thirteen. And, as a man, I've been... I've been *killing* people. Yeah, you heard that right. I am a killer, a murderer, a... a... *a serial killer.*"

Jacob stared at his brother with a deadpan expression, then he burst into a chuckle. *A prank,* he thought, *all of this just for a stupid joke.* He rolled his eyes and shook his head, amused by his brother's confession. Kevin remained serious, though—not a flicker of his eyelids or a twitch of his lips.

Kevin asked, "What? You don't believe me?"

Jacob stopped laughing and stuttered, "N–No. I mean, you–you're kidding, aren't you?"

"No. I'm not kidding. I told you: this is 100-percent true. Here, let me show you something."

Kevin knelt down in front of his brother. He pulled a shoe-box out from under the bed. He placed the ripped shoe-box on his desk, then he shuffled through the interior of the box. The sound of rustling paper and a putrid scent emerged from the interior. He pulled a USB flash drive out of the box.

Kevin said, "Come here. Check this out."

Jacob reluctantly followed his brother's directions. He stood from the bed and approached the desk. He leaned over Kevin's shoulder and stared at the monitor. Fear—unadulterated fear—glittered in his eyes.

Kevin had already opened a folder stored on the flash drive. He slowly scrolled down the folder, revealing a seemingly endless trove of obscene materials—high-quality pictures and high-definition footage of evil and deviance.

His head covered with a ski mask, Kevin appeared in most of the content. In one photo, he appeared to be watching as an old tool shed burned to the ground. In another photo, he posed next to a mutilated dog who was lynched—hanging from the side of a brick wall. There was even some footage of himself chasing a cat down a desolate street, repeatedly stabbing it.

Have you ever heard an innocent animal yelp? It was one of the most excruciating sounds to the human ear.

Kevin's violence wasn't restricted to old buildings and small animals. He posed next to dead bodies in countless photos, too. A short video even showed him kissing the cheek of a deceased homeless woman, then he licked and sucked on her ear. Another clip depicted him urinating on a homeless man's crushed head—a bloodied aluminum baseball bat rolling on the floor near the body.

Smirking, Kevin tapped the screen and explained, "At night, at least once a month, I sneak out of the house and go over to Skid Row. You know, the place with all of those abandoned buildings. Some people call it the 'No-Light District,' since it's completely abandoned. I go over there and I... I have some fun. I play with the stray animals, I make 'love' to a few whores, and I kill the homeless people. I take pictures, I shoot videos... I make mementos because I *need* them. All of this would be pointless if I just forgot about it, right?"

Jacob didn't respond. He *couldn't* respond. His vocabulary was wiped by the shocking revelation. He absently stared at the monitor, lost in a storm of muddled thoughts.

Kevin said, "Let me show you something else."

He reached into the shoe-box, then he pulled out a glass jar without a label. The jar used to hold pickles in the fridge. There were no pickles in the jar, though. Instead, the human teeth of Kevin's victims floated in rancid water inside of the jar. Some of the teeth looked rotten, others looked fresh.

As he shook the jar, causing the teeth to *clink* as they crashed into each other, Kevin said, "I try to pull out at least one tooth from each person I kill. I use pliers or a knife to do it. Sometimes, the teeth just fall out with a kick to the face. The homeless... they don't have great dental coverage. I'd keep 'em in milk, but I don't have a fridge in here, so... This is good enough. Awesome, isn't it?"

Jacob gazed at the jar, appalled. He stepped in reverse and backed away from his brother. He fell back onto the bed. He opened his mouth to speak, but he couldn't utter a word. The entire situation was surreal to him—a horrific nightmare.

Jacob asked, "Why? Why are you telling me this? Why are you... Why are you confessing to me or whatever? This is fucked up, man. It's so fucked up..."

Kevin responded, "This isn't a confession, Jacob. If you confess to something, that means you did something wrong. Like I said, other people might think I'm doing 'bad' things, but I don't think so. I'm just living my life without rules. That's all."

"S–So... Why did you show me all of this?"

"It's an offer. It's a... a proposal. I want you to join me. I know you love animals, so we don't have to 'play' with them. We can play with fire instead. And, when we're not playing with fire, we can *kill*. Sounds good, doesn't it?"

No—the word was clogged in Jacob's throat. He thought about screaming for his mother, but he didn't want to interrupt her sex. He wanted to avoid that awkward situation. Besides, his curiosity got the best of him.

Teary-eyed, Jacob asked, "Why? Wh–Why do you want me?"

"I'm bored. I'm sick and tired of working by myself. I'm tired of killing homeless people. I mean, no one cares about them so it's pointless. It's fun, but... it's just pointless, little man. If I want to do something bigger, I'm going to need help luring riskier targets. That's where you come in. You can–"

"*No.* I can't do it. I–I'm not a killer. This is... Shit, this is crazy!"

"Hey, keep your voice down, idiot," Kevin said as he glanced over at the door. He leaned forward in his seat, moving closer to his younger brother. He said, "Listen, I understand why you're scared. I get it, man. I was scared, too. You have to learn how to free your mind, though. Read my lips, Jacob: we're not doing anything bad. Killing people... It's part of human nature. The government has... has *twisted* the way the world works. They force us to go to school just to teach us how to obey *their* rules. Rules we never really had a chance to make in the first place. We're brainwashed into thinking things are good or bad when none of that shit exists. Animals have been killing each other since the beginning of time... It's natural. Killing is fun and rewarding, Jacob. Trust me."

Jacob shook his head and murmured, "What the hell? This... This isn't happening. Oh, shit..."

He lurched towards the door, slipping and sliding on the dirty laundry. He frantically shook the door knob, but the door wouldn't budge. He felt as if he were trapped by a mystical force in a dungeon with a serial killer. He examined the knob. *The lock,* he thought, *it's just the lock.* He wasn't thinking straight so he forgot Kevin had locked the door.

He turned the lock and opened the door, then he exited the room. He held his hands over his ears and cried as he returned to his bedroom. He didn't want to hear his mother's moans, he didn't want to remember his brother's words. He slammed the door behind him, then he hopped onto his bed and wrapped his pillow around his head.

As he curled into the fetal position, tears streaming down his rosy cheeks, Jacob said, "It's not real, it's not real, it's *not* real..."

In his bedroom, Kevin closed his door and whispered, "You'll come around..."

He smiled and shook his head, tickled by their encounter. He wasn't bothered by his brother's negative reaction. He planted a seed in Jacob's mind and he planned on allowing it to flourish with time. He returned to the closet, closing the door behind him.

Chapter Three

Breakfast

Jacob stood in the kitchen archway, his backpack slung over his shoulder. He glanced around the room, as if he didn't recognize his own home. Like the rest of the house, the kitchen was small, dark, and grimy. The walls were dark and stained, the linoleum floor was cracked and mucky. A cockroach occasionally skittered across the countertops, searching for shelter in the filthy kitchen.

Kevin already sat at the kitchen table, nonchalantly eating his cereal. He didn't appear concerned about his confession during the previous night.

Jacob thought: *maybe it was all a nightmare, maybe he was just messing around, maybe he just doesn't care.* He had trouble reading his brother's enigmatic demeanor. He approached the table and poured himself a bowl of cereal.

He asked, "Is that guy gone yet?" Kevin filled his mouth with a spoonful of cereal and nodded. Jacob sat down across from his brother and said, "About last night... Was all of that fake? Were you serious about the–"

"Not now," Kevin interrupted.

As she walked into the kitchen, Isabel smiled and said, "Good morning, boys." She patted Kevin's shoulder and asked, "Did you heat up some water for coffee?"

Without looking up from his bowl, Kevin responded, "Yeah. It's ready."

"Thanks, hun."

Kevin watched as Isabel walked to the stove. His mother wore a purple satin nightgown—nothing more, nothing less. Her large breasts jiggled with the slightest movement. Her gown rose every time she leaned over the counter, revealing her firm ass. Of course, after a night of wild sex, she forgot to wear underwear.

Jacob stared at Kevin with a furrowed brow, stunned by his deviance. His brother blatantly leered at their mother. He couldn't say a word about it.

As she prepared her coffee, Isabel said, "Sorry if I kept you up last night. I was watching a movie and I ended up falling asleep without turning it off. I mean, I was *knocked* out. I must have been exhausted after the party."

Kevin asked, "What were you watching?"

"Hmm? Oh, it was just a movie. Whatever was on last night."

"A movie? It sounded like porn to me."

Isabel shook her head and rolled her eyes. She took a sip of her coffee, then she said, "It wasn't a porno or anything like that, Kev. It was just a movie. Movies are filled with sex nowadays. So, that's probably what you heard: a sex scene."

Kevin snickered as he shoved another spoonful of cereal into his mouth. Like an obnoxious child, his mother stuck to her excuse in spite of the overwhelming evidence against her. The shoe was on the other foot.

Kevin asked, "What about that guy, mom?"

Rosy-cheeked, Isabel stuttered, "G–Guy? Wha–What guy?"

"That guy from the party. You know, the guy who didn't go home until two in the morning. We're not blind."

Isabel frowned and sighed in disappointment. She leaned back on the counter and crossed her arms. She vacantly stared at her coffee. Although she was a lustful woman, she wasn't comfortable talking about sex around her children. The subject was always difficult to tackle, especially when a mother had to admit to sexual relationships with men who weren't her husband.

Isabel said, "Listen, I don't want to make this into a big deal. That man was just one of... one of mommy's friends. We spent the night... Well, we spent the night together. That's all you have to know about that. Like I said, I'm sorry about the noise. It won't happen again."

The boys stared at their distraught mother. Jacob was indifferent, Kevin was delighted. They continued eating their cereal, munching on the toasted oats and slurping the milk.

Isabel took another sip of her coffee, then she said, "Anyway, I have to head out to work soon. I'm going to shower, grab a quick bite to eat, then I'll leave. I'm not sure if we have the time, but I might be able to give you guys a ride to school if you want to wait."

Kevin responded, "No, it's okay. I'm going to walk Jacob to school today, then I'll walk to my school. We have to leave now, though. It's getting late."

"Okay, that sounds good. Have a nice day at school. Bring your plates over and I'll wash 'em for you."

Isabel turned towards the sink and turned on the faucet. As she waited for the water to heat up, she poured some dish soap on the sponge and stared down at the sink. There was already a stack of dirty dishes in the sink. She wasn't going to wash all of the dishes, though. *After work,* she thought, *this time, I'll actually clean this whole place up.*

Jacob placed his bowl and spoon on the counter near the sink, then he stood on his tiptoes and kissed his mother's cheek—she was still a few inches taller than him after all. He grabbed his backpack from the floor, then he walked to the archway and waited for his brother.

Kevin stopped directly behind his mother. He leaned over her and placed his bowl on the counter next to the sink. As he reached for the counter, he rubbed his crotch on his mother's ass. He smirked as he moved up and down, shamelessly grinding on his own mother. He even leaned back and leered at her ass.

Isabel nervously giggled, surprised by Kevin's inappropriate actions. At first, she thought it was an innocent mistake—he stumbled forward and accidentally rubbed himself on her. She had felt men grinding on her ass before, though. She stopped laughing as soon as she felt his penis growing in his jeans.

Isabel slinked away from the sink and escaped Kevin's grip. She turned around and glared at her son—nervous, shocked, *angry*. She didn't dare glance down at his crotch.

In a stern tone, Isabel said, "Don't do that again, Kevin White. I'm not going to play these nasty games with you. Do you understand me, young man?"

Kevin stared at his mother with a fierce, icy glare. He appeared to be infuriated by the rejection. Before his mother could utter another word, he cracked a smile and shrugged.

He grabbed his backpack from the kitchen table and said, "Sorry about that, mom. It was just an accident. I slipped, okay? I'll try to keep my balance next time... or maybe I'll just let myself fall so I can hit my head on the counter."

Isabel stuttered, "D–Don't say that. It–It's okay. You... You should get going now. I'll see you after work."

Kevin grinned and said, "Okay. Love you, mom."

"I love you, too..."

Kevin patted Jacob's shoulder and said, "Let's get out of here, little man. We wouldn't want to be late to school, right?"

Jacob reluctantly followed his brother to the front door. He took one final glance at his mother. She looked flustered and frustrated, but he couldn't offer her any words of reassurance. He walked out of the house and closed the door behind him.

Chapter Four

Before School

The brothers lived at the end of the circular cul-de-sac in the impoverished side of town. The rest of the neighborhood was comprised of small, tumbledown houses. Some of the houses were even abandoned and condemned. Yet, despite their financial hardships, the people seemed happy in the close-knit community. The siblings strolled down the tree-lined sidewalk and headed north to their schools.

Jacob was an eighth grader at the local middle school, Kevin was a senior at the local high school. Fortunately for the brothers, their schools were located on the same block. Unfortunately for the siblings, graduation day was around the corner. They wouldn't be close to each other after they graduated.

As they walked, Jacob glanced up at the overcast sky and asked, "What was up with that thing you did to mom in the kitchen? Did you, like... *grind* on her or something?"

"Grind?" Kevin repeated in an uncertain tone.

"Yeah. Grinding, you know? It's when a girl rubs her ass on a guy's lap or whatever. I saw it at school once. I guess some girls were 'twerking' or something and–"

"I know what 'grinding' is," Kevin interrupted. "I

don't want you to worry about me or mom, Jacob. Like I said, I just slipped and fell on her. You'll understand everything else when you're older. Forget about it for now."

Jacob stared at his brother with a raised brow. *You'll understand everything else when you're older* —the simple statement confused him. He understood the idea of 'slipping.' People slipped all the time so it wasn't a difficult concept to comprehend. He believed his brother was referring to something sexual. *He really was grinding on her,* he thought.

The younger sibling lowered his head and grimaced in disgust. Although he wasn't aware of the term, incest made him feel nauseous. Instead of tackling his brother's sexual deviance, he decided to change the subject.

Jacob said, "About last night..."

Kevin asked, "Did you think about my offer?"

"To be honest, I've been trying to forget about it. It's hard, though. Whenever I close my eyes, I see those pictures. You... You're fucked up, Kevin."

"No, I'm not fucked up. I think I'm one of the normal ones around here. You see, I embrace human nature in its *purest* form," Kevin explained. He pulled his knockoff cell phone out of his pocket. He wagged the device at his brother and said, "Human nature isn't supposed to be about phones and computers. It's not supposed to be about good and bad. Being human means being a survivor. And, in order to survive, you have to wipe out everyone who's weaker than you... and everyone who's stronger. You move up until you're at the top of the food chain and *everyone* is scared of you. So, I'm not fucked up. I'm just human, little man."

Jacob slowed his pace and walked a few steps behind his older brother. Hundreds of thoughts stampeded across his mind. *Is there really no such thing as good or bad? Are we supposed to be killing each other?*–he thought. He didn't find the answers to his questions, but he was truly amazed by Kevin's passionate speech. He jogged to catch up to his brother.

Kevin nudged Jacob's arm and asked, "Have you seriously never thought about killing someone before? Shit, man, when I was in kindergarten, I used to think about stabbing my teacher's neck with a pencil. I thought about drowning my swimming teacher when I was in third grade. I even tried to do it, but that idiot thought I was just playing. 'Boys will be boys,' you know? Come on, Jacob. You've thought about it, haven't you?"

Jacob sighed and rubbed the nape of his neck, anxious. The question was actually common— drunks had been asking that question for centuries —but it was difficult to answer due to the special circumstances. He was talking to a *real* serial killer after all. However, at heart, he knew the answer: *yes, I wish I could kill.*

Kevin smiled as he glanced over at his younger brother. He spotted the uncertainty in Jacob's eyes. The boy was malleable.

Kevin said, "I knew it." Jacob turned towards Kevin with wide eyes, as if to say: *wait, what?* Kevin said, "You've thought about it before. You know, I think it runs in the family."

"No, Kev. Killing is... is wrong. Everyone knows that."

"We've been through this before, little man. Good, bad... None of that shit matters. And, even if it did, it's not fair to say 'killing is bad.' That's like saying 'all black people are criminals' or 'all white people like fucking their family members.' Like crime and incest, it's a case-by-case thing. Think of it this way: killing isn't bad during war, right? Killing isn't bad when someone's trying to protect his family from a crazy robber, right?"

But, you kill innocent animals and people—Jacob fought the urge to blurt out the response. He didn't want to challenge his brother. He didn't know how he would respond.

Kevin grinned as he caught a glimpse of an old house at the corner of the street. The house belonged to the friendly neighborhood pedophile—Dean 'Sweets' Murray.

Dean was a balding middle-aged man who kept to himself. He took care of his front lawn, he reported crimes at the first sign of trouble, but he rarely spoke to his neighbors—and his neighbors rarely spoke to him. He was known around the neighborhood as 'Sweets' because he was always eating candy. The nickname seemed to follow him throughout his life, though. Due to his addiction to sweets, one of his top canine teeth was rotten— black and putrid.

As expected, Dean stood on his front lawn and

watered his freshly-mown grass. He wore a plain t-shirt, mesh shorts, and flip flops. He appeared lethargic and depressed.

Kevin shoved Jacob and said, "Say 'hi' to Sweets."

"What? Why?"

"Just do it. Trust me, it's going to be worth it."

Jacob didn't have the opportunity to consider his options. The siblings reached the sex offender's house.

Jacob leaned over the short chain-link fence and said, "Hey, Sweets."

Dean furrowed his brow and cocked his head back, shocked by the boy's greeting. He was usually ignored or berated by the community. He lifted his arm to wave, but he stopped himself before his hand reached his chest.

In a society of justifiably protective people, a wave from a convicted sex offender was equivalent to an inappropriate touch. He didn't want to incriminate himself. He turned his attention to his hose and continued watering his lawn.

As they strolled down the sidewalk, Jacob asked, "Why'd you want me to do that?"

Kevin said, "Dean is a bad man. He's a pedophile. He fucked little kids in the past. We both know that. Nowadays, he claims he's 'rehabilitated.' You know what that means, right?" Jacob shrugged. Kevin explained, "It means he *pretends* like he doesn't like little kids anymore. He *pretends* like he's seen the... the error of his ways. That's not true, though. He's still a pervert. He knows it, I know it, everyone knows it... And, since he knows it, he tries to keep to himself because he doesn't want to fall to his urges. So, he doesn't really trust anyone. You just planted a seed in his fucked up little head—a seed of trust. We've got him where we want him."

Jacob shook his head and said, "I don't understand."

"It's simple: he's going to be our first victim together. You just started baiting him for us."

Jacob stopped walking. He stared at his brother with wide eyes, awed by his audacity. His older brother didn't stop, though. He kept walking, unperturbed by his own plans of murder. Again, Jacob jogged to catch up to his brother.

He stuttered, "N–No. I... I told you already: I *can't* do that. I'm not a killer."

"Don't worry about that. I'm going to make you a killer and you're going to thank me for it. Besides, I know you can do it. And, you *will* do it because I can see it in you."

"See it in me? See what?"

"I see anger in your eyes. I see hatred in your soul—if you believe in that sorta thing. It's the same hatred I felt for this fucked up world when I first started killing. You and me, Jacob... We're the same. We're the rotten apples that fell from the family tree."

Jacob frowned and lowered his head, ashamed. His brother wasn't lying. At only thirteen years old, he already hated the world. Resentment festered in his heart and envy poisoned his mind. He hated everyone and everything because he was dealt a bad hand. Life was never fair to him.

Kevin continued, "It's a good thing we're starting with him, too. Dean is the worst type of weakling on this planet. Instead of raping women, he rapes kids. Weak people like him don't deserve to live. If you want an example of 'bad,' well there it is. He's bad, Jacob, not me. We'd be doing the world a favor by getting rid of him. Don't think of it as murder, think of it as justice."

Kevin smiled and nodded as the thought dawned onto him—*justice.* He had to ease his brother into becoming a serial killer by sugarcoating his actions.

He said, "Yeah, that's what I'm talking about. Sometimes, murder is justified. War, law enforcement, self-defense... Trust me, Dean is the type of guy that deserves to die. He's living here, all peaceful and shit, but he could hurt another kid at any moment. He could even be planning to hurt your little girlfriend, Molly. You wouldn't want that, would you?"

Jacob shook his head and said, "She's not my girlfriend."

"It doesn't matter. You know I'm right. Some people deserve to die. That's all I'm trying to say. Okay?"

The siblings stopped at a crosswalk. Jacob stared at his brother as he thought about his speech and perspective. He glanced down at his sneakers as he considered Kevin's justifications. It made sense to him, too. *Some people deserve to die,* he thought, *but do we deserve to kill?* He agreed with his brother's viewpoint of the world, but he still wasn't fond of murder.

Kevin beckoned to Jacob and said, "Come on. We'll talk about it later. We're going to be late for school."

Jacob shook his head and snapped out of his trance. Lost in his thoughts, he didn't notice the light had changed. He jogged across the crosswalk and followed his brother to their schools.

As he jogged, he whispered, "We'll talk about it later..."

Chapter Five

A Regular Day at School

Jacob stared at the wall as he pissed in the urinal. Crude drawings of male genitalia and gang names were scraped into the tiles. The stall to his left didn't fare any better—vandalized with notes and drawings. The sound of urine streaming across the urinal was accompanied by a humming sound from the lights. A plopping sound occasionally emerged from the sinks behind him.

The student was alone in the restroom. He was abandoned by the world, left alone with his horrifying thoughts. His brother's sinister words echoed through his mind—*some people deserve to die.* Images of Kevin's violent actions flashed in his mind, too. His vision was covered with specks of blood. His brain throbbed, his heart pounded, his legs wobbled.

Jacob tightly closed his eyes and muttered, "Shit..." With his eyes closed, he zipped his pants up and shook his head. He opened his eyes and whispered, "I have to forget about it."

He turned around and walked towards the sinks. As he walked past the stall wall, he was viciously pushed by Wyatt. He stumbled until he hit the wall at the farthest end of the restroom. He leaned on the wall and stared back at his bully, wide-eyed. He didn't even hear him enter the restroom.

Wyatt snickered as he rubbed his nose, blatantly proud of himself. David and Eric, his entourage of bullies, stood behind him—laughing and muttering.

Wyatt asked, "What are you doing in here by yourself, Jacob? You looking for a gloryhole or something? You want to choke on some cock like your mom? I heard she uses that glory hole over at Sam's Gas Station. I think she likes that BBC, but she'll take anything, won't she?" Jacob lowered his head and clenched his jaw, struggling to contain his rage. Wyatt chuckled, then he asked, "What's the matter? Are you mad at me? Is that it? You don't like it when I talk about your mom? Or were you really looking for some cock, you little faggot?"

What was the best way to deal with a vicious bully? Jacob had tried reasoning with Wyatt before, but it didn't work. He tried to fight back, blindly swinging and kicking at him, but the bully was too strong. Watching Jacob fight Wyatt was like watching a cowardly chihuahua fight an aggressive lion—it was horrifying.

So, Jacob opted for the safest bet: walk away and pretend like nothing happened. He took a deep breath, then he walked around his bullies. To his dismay, he only made it two steps past the group before Wyatt ran in front of him and blocked his path again. Of course, David and Eric also surrounded him.

Jacob took a step in reverse. Without making eye contact, he asked, "Can you please let me leave?"

Wyatt said, "Of course, buddy."

As Jacob took a step to his left, Wyatt took a step

to his right—still blocking his path.

Wyatt asked, "What? Aren't you going to wash your hands?"

Jacob stared at his bully and frowned. His disappointed facial expression said: *are you serious right now?* He sighed, then he turned towards the sink.

Before he could turn the handle, Wyatt grabbed Jacob's wrist and said, "Not like that. Get down on your knees and put your hands in front of you."

"My–My knees?"

"Yeah, your knees. Get down there like when you're sucking dick. You've probably seen your mom do it before. Then, put your hands out like this."

Wyatt moved his hands in front of his chest with his hands cupped as if he were begging for an extra bowl of soup. Jacob couldn't predict his bully's wicked plans.

Jacob asked, "What are you going to do?"

Wyatt glanced over at Eric and said, "Eric's going to piss on your hands to make sure they're *squeaky* clean."

Jacob grimaced in disgust. He took another step in reverse. He glanced to his left, then to his right. There was no escape. He could see the door a few meters behind his bullies, past the stalls and sinks. If he couldn't reach the door, he could only hope a teacher would walk into the restroom and interrupt the confrontation.

In a condescending tone, Wyatt asked, "What's the matter, Jacob? You act like you've never pissed on your hands before. I mean, let's be real, man. You're the poorest kid in school. You probably don't even wash your hands at home. Shit, man, you probably don't even have water at your house. Come on, let Eric piss on your hands."

Jacob sniffled and stuttered, "N–No..."

"*No?* You've got to be kidding me. I'm giving you a chance to get your hands washed with some grade-A piss and you say 'no?' I should have expected that. You and your fucking hooker mom don't know anything about respect. Your punk-ass brother is the same, too. He just hides all day like a bitch."

Yeah, you're right—the entourage of bullies mumbled their approval of Wyatt's bullying. They stroked their leader's ego. Jacob couldn't muster the courage to respond. Since he couldn't walk *around* the thugs, he tried to walk through them. Wyatt pushed him back, causing Jacob to stumble in reverse until he hit the wall.

Wyatt sternly said, "Not until you wash your damn hands."

Eyes welling over with tears, Jacob rushed to the sink and reached for the handle.

Wyatt pushed him away and shouted, "With the piss, bitch!"

Jacob staggered to his knees in front of the bullies. He whimpered as he stared down at the linoleum floor. In order to escape from the restroom without a beating, he had to comply. He truly felt like he didn't have any other options. His arms trembled as he lifted his hands up to his chest with his palms facing the ceiling.

As he nudged Eric's arm, Wyatt smirked and said, "Do it. Wash this faggot's hands."

As he walked in front of Jacob and reached for his waistband, Eric said, "Alright. Just don't suck on it, Jacob."

Jacob closed his eyes as Eric unzipped his pants. The sound of the zipper *crackling* caused him to shudder. He panted and winced as he felt the warm piss splashing on his hands. He could hear the bullies laughing hysterically over his heavy breathing. *Hurry up and finish,* he thought.

Bullies enjoyed changing the rules, though.

Eric adjusted his aim and pissed on Jacob's face. The urine splashed on his hair, forehead, nose, cheeks, and lips. A few drops of the pungent fluid even landed in his mouth. Some of the piss dripped onto his black t-shirt, too.

Jacob fell back on his ass as he coughed and retched. He felt vomit clogging his throat, ready to eject from his mouth like puke in a horror movie. He waved his arms, causing more urine to splatter on the floor. The bullies laughed, finding joy in their inappropriate behavior.

As Eric zipped up his pants, Wyatt grinned and shouted, "Damn, man! I told you to wash his hands, I didn't tell you to give him a fucking golden shower!"

Eric shrugged and said, "My bad."

"You're fucking sick, dude," David remarked.

As the boys walked towards the exit, Wyatt asked, "Aren't you going to wash your hands, Eric?"

Eric responded, "Fuck that."

Although the bullies had already exited the

restroom, Jacob could still hear them laughing about the confrontation. Tears streaming down his cheeks, he rushed to the sinks. He vigorously rubbed his hands and face with hot water, trying his best to clean himself before his next class. He spit and retched, too, disgusted by the taste of urine.

As he washed himself, Jacob muttered, "You're going to pay for this, Wyatt. I swear, you're all going to pay..."

***

Jacob sat at the back of his math class—the last seat in the last row. He scraped the surface of his desk with his number-two pencil as he thought about the brutal bullying he endured. Fortunately for him, Wyatt wasn't in his class. Yet, he still felt like everyone was looking at him—*mocking him.*

The fact was difficult to admit: he reeked of urine. The scent of ammonia was slight but noticeable. The cool breeze blowing through the open windows wafted the scent across the classroom. The stench meandered into the neighboring nostrils, causing the students' noses to scrunch.

Some of the students didn't notice, others didn't care. However, Jacob felt like *everyone* could smell the piss on his shirt. The more he thought about the stench, the stronger it grew. He could still taste the urine in his mouth, too.

Barely negligible, Jacob muttered, "Shit... Why does this always happen to me? What did I do to deserve this? Fucking assholes..."

The blonde girl in the seat in front of him turned

around. She usually avoided contact with Jacob, but she didn't have a choice. She sneered in disgust as she placed a sheet of paper on Jacob's desk. As she turned forward in her seat, the girl muttered about Jacob's gross stench. She said something along the lines of: *you're so nasty, go home and take a shower.* The snide remark caused another student to chuckle.

Jacob ignored the petty insults—*the same ol' shit.* He stared down at the sheet of paper. It was a graded quiz. The quiz had twenty questions. He answered thirteen of the questions incorrectly, which left him with an F-grade at 35-percent. He wasn't disappointed, though. He had already failed multiple tests so he wasn't expecting a passing grade. He glanced up at the front of the class.

Mr. Sullivan, his teacher, walked up to the whiteboard after he passed out the last stack of quizzes. The middle-aged man ran his fingers through the thin graying hair on the sides of his head, barely avoiding the bald spot at the center of his dome. He muttered to himself as he adjusted his button-up shirt and tie.

Sullivan asked, "Did I miss anyone? Do you all have your tests?" The class responded with different variations of the same answer: *yes, yeah, yep.* Sullivan nodded and said, "Good, good. Most of you did very well on this quiz. I believe we had a few 100-percent scores this time around. I'm very proud of that. Like I said: if you do your homework, if you spend *at least* thirty minutes studying after school, you'll do fine in my class. It seems like a few of you didn't listen to that advice, though."

He placed his hands on his hips and stared at the back of the class. He shook his head as he glanced over at Jacob and the other slackers.

He sighed in disappointment, then he said, "I won't be grading on a curve this time. I've tried to help some of you before, but you're still not listening. You don't seem to care about your grades, but I know someone who does."

The class *oohed* and *awwed,* entertained by the drama. A few of the students even pulled their phones out, hoping to capture a heated confrontation or a moment of embarrassment. They had been in the class before, so they knew how their teacher worked.

Sullivan shouted, "Jacob!"

Jacob bit his bottom lip and leaned back in his seat. *I knew he was going to call on me,* he thought, *he always picks on me.* He stared back at his teacher, his cheeks redder than an apple.

Sullivan said, "This is the... the *eighth* test you've failed this semester. You've outdone yourself this time. I think you hold the record for the most lowest-graded quizzes in the class—and that's not something to be proud of. You're not turning in your homework, you're not paying attention in class... I have to try something else." He turned his attention to the rest of the class and asked, "Since I'm not able to get through to him, would anyone like to tutor Jacob for extra-credit? Anyone? I'll boost your grade up by three-percent at the end of the semester."

Anxious, Jacob glanced around the classroom.

The students whispered among themselves, some stared back at Jacob with grimaces of disgust, but no one volunteered. The spotlight was placed on him so he was publicly shunned and humiliated.

Truth be told, he felt the urge to cry in class. He had to stop himself from breaking down, though. Crying would only worsen the bullying.

Sullivan sighed again, then he said, "Okay. The offer will be on the table for the rest of the week. I know some of you can use the extra credit and I know Jacob could really use the help. Talk to me after class if you're interested." He glanced over at Jacob and said, "Jacob, I'm calling your mother after class. At this rate, you're going to be held back. We need to do something about this. Math is a pillar of your education and, if you don't build on it or reinforce it, everything will collapse. Remember that."

Jacob lowered his head in shame. He didn't care about the call to his mother. He was more concerned about the public humiliation. He thought about his teacher's intentions. The man could have talked to him privately after class, but he used Jacob to set an example instead.

His classmates laughed at his pain. A few of them even took pictures and recorded Jacob, hoping to get 'likes' on Facebook and Instagram. They hoped to gain popularity by creating the next viral 'meme.' Public shaming was popular among the younger generation.

Sullivan tapped his marker on the board and said, "Enough of that. Come on, quiet down and put your phones away." The kids continued laughing and talking amongst themselves. Sullivan sternly said, "*Stop it.* Some of you shouldn't be laughing anyway. I'm calling your parents, too. Now, quiet down and focus."

The students listened to their teacher and the chatter dwindled to a few whispers. Class continued at its regular pace, led by Sullivan's monotonous voice.

Jacob stared down at his quiz. A tear dripped from his eye and plopped on the paper as he blinked. He looked away from his classmates, refusing to show weakness in the toxic school environment. He clenched his fists and struggled to control himself. One word echoed through his mind: *vengeance.*

***

In the school quad, Jacob sat by his lonesome at a table. His classmates didn't want to share a table with the student who smelled like piss—and he couldn't blame them. He sighed in disappointment as he stared down at his microwaved burrito. Thinking about his horrible day caused him to lose his appetite. He pushed the foam tray forward, then he glanced around the quad.

Although some would argue otherwise, middle school was similar to high school—the schedules, the subjects, the teachers, *the cliques.* During lunch, students sat in isolated clusters on the benches and tables. Jocks sat with jocks, cheerleaders sat with cheerleaders, nerds sat with nerds, and so on. Once a clique was formed, new recruits were rarely accepted.

Jacob frowned as he watched his classmates. He was sincerely hurt by their smiles. Their laughter—soft and innocent—sounded like a shrill alarm to him. Their happiness caused him nothing but pain. He thought: *why can't I be happy like them? Why don't they ever invite me to eat with them?* The answer was simple—and he knew that very well.

Life wasn't a made-for-TV anti-bullying movie.

As the epiphany dawned onto him, Jacob's frown turned into a scowl. He realized that he despised his classmates. He hated the cheerleaders and jocks because of their seemingly perfect qualities and their rotten attitudes. He loathed the rich students who took notes on their iPads while his family struggled to afford notebooks and pencils. He disliked the geeks, too.

Geeks and outcasts were supposed to stick together, but they never helped him. He didn't belong with the bullies, either.

Through his gritted teeth, Jacob whispered, "Fuck 'em. I don't need anyone."

There were still fifteen minutes left until lunch ended. He thought about staying at the table for the remainder of the period, but he couldn't control his anxiety. He was afraid he would snap at one of his classmates or teachers if they looked at him with the wrong expression.

He shoved the tray into the neighboring trash can, then he marched away from the table—infuriated. He walked towards the back of the outdoor school, past the classrooms and library. The quad was the busiest area during lunch, so he figured he would find some peace in the basketball courts.

As he walked past the cliques and couples, Jacob sneered and whispered, "Fuck you, fuck you, fuck you..."

He clenched his fists, digging his fingernails into his palms. He kept his composure, though. He walked past a chain-link fence and found himself in an outdoor activity area. His athletic peers played basketball on the courts and soccer on the fields. He walked alongside the fence and headed to the other side of the school.

"Shit," Jacob muttered. He spotted Wyatt playing basketball with a few students. He lowered his head and whispered, "Just ignore him..."

Before he could reach the exit, a basketball struck the side of his head—*thud!* Jacob teetered left-and-right, caught off guard by the blow. He wasn't exactly dazed—it was a basketball, not a bowling ball—but he was surprised. He thought Wyatt would have already reached his daily bullying quota.

Jacob turned and glared at Wyatt. A fire of fury burned in his livid eyes, rage surged across each of his limbs. Yet, he couldn't say a word.

Wyatt scowled at Jacob and asked, "What's wrong with you, you fuckin' piss-guzzler? What are you going to do, faggot?"

Jacob imagined himself stabbing Wyatt with his number-two pencil. If he sharpened it enough, he could stab his bully's flabby stomach or penetrate his thick neck. Then, he could bounce the basketball on his face until his nose was pushed into his skull. It was all a fantasy, though. He could never beat Wyatt in a one-on-one fight, so he surely wouldn't win with the other bullies around.

Jacob took a deep breath and recomposed himself. He turned and walked away from the court. *Three steps*—he only took three measly steps before he was stopped again.

Wyatt shouted, "Pass the ball back, idiot! Have some respect, man!"

Jacob responded, "You threw it. Why don't–"

"And you didn't catch it," Wyatt interrupted. "Pass the ball or we're going to beat the shit out of you. Fuck, man, we might even shit on you this time. You've already got Eric's piss all over you so you might like his shit, too. You want a fudge bath, faggot?"

The boys laughed and high-fived, amused by the obscene threat. Wyatt was serious, though. The bullies would really defecate on Jacob if he didn't comply. Fighting the urge to cry, Jacob sighed and shook his head. He grabbed the basketball from beside the chain-link fence. He tossed the ball at Wyatt and the other players, then he walked away.

Again, before he could reach the exit, the basketball hit the side of Jacob's head. He didn't have to turn back to know who threw the ball. Wyatt's obnoxious laughter danced into his ears. His cackle was accompanied by the laughter of the other onlookers. Bullying appeared to be celebrated until the bullied committed suicide or shot up a school; then, they would all pretend to be sad and remorseful.

The bell rang, echoing across the school.

Tears streaming down his cheeks, Jacob ran away from the basketball courts with his head down. He didn't run straight to class, though. He headed to a restroom to wipe his face and recompose himself. He didn't care about his inevitable tardiness. The bullying, the humiliation, the failure—it was all part of a regular day at school for Jacob.

Chapter Six

After School

Kevin casually leaned on the front gate of the middle school, his backpack slung over his shoulder. He stared at the outdoor campus, patiently waiting for school to end. Waiting to pick up their children, parents watched the teenager from the safety of their vehicles—blatantly suspicious. A young adult dressed in all black didn't paint a pretty picture to overprotective parents. Although they wouldn't admit it, the concerned parents shared the same thought: *a school shooter?*

Kevin chuckled and shook his head, tickled by the attention. He reached into his backpack and acted as if he were looking for something. He wanted to scare the judgmental parents by acting like he was reaching for something—and it worked. The adults pulled their phones out and started dialing 911. Some even opened their car doors, ready to tackle the teenager at the first sign of trouble.

The trouble-making student pulled his hand out of the bag. Of course, he was empty-handed. He smirked and shrugged—*oops.* The bell rang.

He stepped aside and watched as the young students poured out of the school. Some of the kids ran to the bus stops, others rushed to their parents' cars, and a few walked home. Most of the students appeared happy and innocent. They gossiped and they bickered, they pushed and they argued, but they didn't seem angry.

Kevin was amused by their innocence. He couldn't help but wonder if they were being taught the truth about the cruel world. *Do they know that they're all going to die and no one is going to care?*– he thought. Regardless, it wasn't his job to teach them about the world. That was up to their parents and older siblings. He only cared about Jacob.

As the crowd thinned, he walked away from the gate and gazed into the gated school. He tilted his head upon spotting his younger brother near the fountain in front of the school.

Wyatt pushed Jacob with all of his might, which caused Jacob to fall to his knees near the fountain. Jacob immediately wrapped his arms around his head, prepared to endure a brutal beating. The bullies didn't pummel him, though. Wyatt and his friends chuckled and muttered as they walked past him.

As he staggered to his feet, brushing the dirt off his pants, Jacob spotted his brother near the front gate. He stopped moving—surprised and concerned.

He whispered, "What are you doing here, Kev?"

Jacob continued to pat his dirty clothing as he approached his brother. He tried to walk past him, but Kevin grabbed his shoulder and stopped him.

Kevin asked, "Why didn't you fight back?"

Jacob stuttered, "I–I didn't... I just didn't feel like it."

"Why?"

"I told you: I didn't feel like it."

"Alright. So, why do you smell like piss?"

Jacob sighed, then he asked, "Can we talk about this later? I just want to go home already."

Kevin nodded and responded, "Fine. Start walking."

The brothers strolled down the sidewalk and headed home. They remained quiet until they found some privacy three blocks away from the school.

As he stared straight ahead, Kevin said, "I saw him push you, that fat fuck. Wyatt, right? Wyatt Anderson? I knew his older brother. He tried the same shit on me, too. He'd push me around, he'd jump me with his friends. He even tried to shank me once. I made him stop, though. You can make Wyatt stop, too. You just need to stand up for yourself. Fuck it... We'll deal with him later."

Jacob cocked his head back as he glanced over at his brother, baffled by the ominous threat. *Deal with him later*—coming from a serial killer, that could mean anything from giving Wyatt an atomic wedgie to feeding his corpse to his parents. He didn't confront his brother about the threat, though. At heart, he would be pleased if Wyatt suddenly died or disappeared.

As they turned the corner and continued walking, Jacob asked, "Hey, doesn't your school end, like, fifteen minutes after mine?"

"So?"

"I was just wondering, you know, how did you get to my school so fast?"

"It's simple, Jacob. I ditched during lunch. I was tired of seeing all of those idiots pretending like life was perfect. I didn't want to hear my other teachers bitching at me, either."

"Where did you go?"

"I went to... to visit a few 'friends' at the No-Light District for a few hours. We had some fun."

Kevin's type of 'fun' involved extreme violence against homeless people. Jacob glanced at his brother's hands, searching for even the smallest speck of blood. He wondered if Kevin killed during his truancy.

Jacob said, "I wish I could ditch, too."

"You can. If you want to ditch, just do it."

"I–I don't know how."

"It's easy. I ditched from your school a lot when I was there. I know how to ditch without getting caught. Maybe I'll show you later."

Jacob stuttered, "Y–Yeah, thanks..."

The siblings walked in silence for a few minutes. They were approaching their neighborhood. The beat-up houses, abandoned cars, and dead grass always revealed when they were getting close to home.

As they approached the sex offender's house, Kevin nudged Jacob's arm and said, "Do it again. Give him a compliment this time." Jacob glanced over at the house—Dean sat on a bench on his porch, reading the news on a tablet computer. Kevin whispered, "*Do it.*"

Again, Jacob didn't have the opportunity to consider his options. He knew his brother's intentions, but he was curious. *Can we actually kill him?*–he thought.

Jacob leaned on Dean's fence and enthusiastically said, "Hey, Sweets! The lawn is looking really good. Um... Thanks for keeping it clean."

Dean glanced over at the siblings. He furrowed his brow upon spotting Jacob. The expression on his face read: *are you seriously talking to me?* He stared at the boy with a blank expression, as if he were contemplating his next move, then he cracked a smile. He appeared to be delighted by the attention. He waved at Jacob, his arm trembling uncontrollably.

In a cracking voice, Dean stuttered, "Tha–Thanks, kid."

As they passed the sex offender's house and headed home, Kevin said, "Damn, that was a lot easier than I thought. You already have that pedo wrapped around your finger... We'll get him later, too. Don't worry about that."

As they continued walking, Jacob glanced back at Dean's house. Thoughts of murder ran through his mind—slaughter, mayhem, carnage. The idea of becoming a murderer was slowly growing on him. He didn't say another word. He simply followed his brother back to their house.

Chapter Seven

Punishment

The afternoon was normal at the White household. Jacob sat at the kitchen, eating a microwavable meal. His meal consisted of fried chicken, mashed potatoes, sweet corn, and a chocolate brownie. It wasn't the most nutritious or delicious meal, but it was edible. Kevin leaned on the counter in front of the microwave, a fork in his right hand. He patiently waited for the microwave's *beep* so he could eat.

The sound of the front door *slamming* echoed through the house. Loud, consistent footsteps immediately followed. The brothers glanced over at the archway, curious.

Isabel emerged in the archway. She stood with her arms away from her body, as if she were welcoming a hug. She had just arrived from work, so she still wore her uniform—a blue polo shirt and khaki pants. Her purse dangled from her bicep. Her eyes and mouth were wide open, but she didn't say a word. She was angry and confused, obviously.

The brothers glanced over at each other, then they shared a shrug.

Jacob turned towards his mother and asked, "What?"

"*What?*" Isabel repeated. She huffed and shook her head, astonished. She muttered, "I don't believe this. These kids... These damn kids..."

She walked into the kitchen and tossed her bag on the counter. She paced in front of the table, muttering to herself about her children. The brothers quietly watched her, waiting for her to explain the situation. The microwaved *beeped* three times—Kevin's meal was ready.

Before Kevin could open the microwave, Isabel said, "*Wait.* Don't open that microwave, Kev. We're not eating right now, okay? We have to talk."

Kevin responded, "About what?"

"I received *two* calls while I was at work. That means I was disrupted *twice* while I was supposed to be working, and that makes me look bad. Those calls weren't for me, either. They weren't social calls. They were calls from your damn schools. The first one came from your school, Kevin. A truancy officer—*a cop*—called me because you were ditching. He said that they might take legal action against us. You can end up under control of the court. We could be fined. Do you know how serious that is?"

Kevin stared at his mother with a deadpan expression. He had to fight the urge to chuckle. He lowered his head, creating a semblance of shame.

Isabel turned towards Jacob and said, "I got a call from your school, too. I got a call from Sullivan, your math teacher. You know him, don't you? Judging from the call, I'm not sure if you can even remember his name."

"I know him. I was–"

"*Quiet.* It's not your turn to talk, Jacob," Isabel said, her voice cracking as if she were trying to stop herself from crying. She sighed, then she said, "I'm very disappointed in you. Your teacher said you might be held back because of your grades in his class. You might have to repeat a grade. Kevin didn't have to repeat any grades. I didn't even have to repeat any grades. What is happening to you?"

Disregarding the family dispute, Kevin opened the microwave and hissed as he grabbed the black tray—it was hot. He carried the tray with his fingertips, then he sat down beside his brother. As he took a bite of his fried chicken, he smiled and nodded at his mother, as if to say: *go on, I'm listening.*

Isabel huffed and shook her head, amazed by her son's nonchalant attitude. She opened her mouth to speak, but she couldn't utter a word. She needed a moment to consider her options. She didn't want to hit her kids, but she had to get through to them.

Isabel said, "Both of you are going down the wrong path."

Jacob said, "I'm sorry, mom. I just don't get math and he doesn't–"

"*Quiet,*" Isabel interrupted, glaring at her son. Jacob sucked his lips inward and sank into his seat. Isabel continued, "You're going down the wrong path. If you keep going this way, you'll end up like your father. An alcoholic, drug-addicted bastard. This path will take you straight to hell with him, too. You better believe me."

Kevin shoved a mouthful of mashed potatoes into his mouth as he stared at his mother. He didn't have anything to say. Jacob wanted to apologize to his mother, but he didn't know if he was allowed to speak. So, the youngster remained quiet.

Unfortunately, Isabel *wanted* him to apologize. She took a long pause and waited for them to say something—*anything*—but her children remained quiet. She misinterpreted their confused silence as defiance. Miscommunication could lead to unintended hostility.

Isabel sat down in front of her kids. As she stared down at the table, she said, "I don't know what I'm going to do, but this is your last warning. I don't want any more calls from teachers or cops. I'm... I don't want you to embarrass me again." She glanced up at her kids for a second, then she turned away again. She said, "I can't even look at you right now. Both of you... you remind me of that asshole we called your 'dad.' I'm raising a thug and a slacker. Unbelievable..."

Kevin took a bite of his fried chicken, then he sucked on his greasy fingers. Again, he wasn't bothered by his mother's insult. Jacob, on the other hand, was sincerely offended by her verbal attack. He thought: *you embarrass us, too, mom.*

Isabel sighed, then she said, "I need you to go to your rooms. Take your food with you, too."

Jacob stuttered, "Wh–Why?"

"You're grounded."

"For how long?"

"I don't know. A day, a week... We'll talk about it after I cool down. Just go to your rooms."

The brothers glanced at each other. They grabbed their trays and their forks, then they headed to their bedrooms.

***

Jacob lay in bed, his stiff pillow wrapped around his head. He squirmed on his bed as he struggled to sleep. Like every other night, his mother's sexual moaning arrived with nighttime. Her moans of pleasure were accompanied by a man's loud groaning. That man would occasionally yell at Isabel. He shouted something along the lines of: *you like that, don't you, you dirty whore?!*

Jacob was still young and innocent, so the dirty talk caught him off guard. He was especially surprised by his mother's words. In response to her temporary lover's aggressive questions, Isabel would shout a different variation of the same submissive answer: *yes, daddy, fuck me harder!* The sex was louder and rougher than ever before.

Jacob crawled to the edge of his bed and peeked out the window. He could see the entire cul-de-sac from his bedroom. There were two cars in front of his house—his mother's beat-up sedan in the driveway and a black hatchback parked directly in front of the house. He recognized the hatchback, too. The car belonged to the mailman, who happened to be married.

The youngster turned over on his bed and whispered, "It's midnight and the mailman is fucking my mom. What the hell?"

He stared at the ceiling as he listened to the rough sex. He thought about the bullying he endured from Wyatt. His mother's lewd behavior was often used to bully him. He couldn't help but wonder if his mother was really a prostitute—or maybe she was just a nymphomaniac. He clenched his jaw and whimpered as the idea grew in his mind.

Eyes welling over with tears, he whispered, "I don't know what to think, mom. I love you, but... I feel wrong. I feel dirty. I feel *angry.* Fuck this."

He wiped the tears from his eyes and stood from his bed. He crept out of his room and tiptoed towards Kevin's bedroom, trying his best to ignore the sound of sex. He opened his brother's door and stopped in the doorway.

Yet again, Kevin was nowhere in sight. Only the light from the computer monitor illuminated the room. Another pornographic video played on the screen. The video depicted a young Japanese woman having sex with her teacher and a group of students in a classroom.

His bare feet firmly planted on the floor, Jacob leaned into the room and whispered, "Kevin. Kevin, are you in here? Hello?"

He leaned back and glanced down the hall, wondering if his brother went to the kitchen for a midnight snack. Aside from his mother's moaning, the rest of the house was quiet.

He stared back into the bedroom and said, "Kevin, we need to talk."

Again, there was no response. As Jacob took his first step into the bedroom, the closet door swung open. Kevin emerged from the closet, lifting his pajama pants up to his waist. He appeared to be out of breath, sweat glistening on his lean body.

Kevin asked, "What are you doing here? What do you want?"

Jacob glanced over at the closet door with a set of inquisitive eyes. *It's none of my business,* he thought, *but what do I say to him?* He shambled into the room, closing the door behind him. He sat at the foot of his brother's bed and twiddled his thumbs.

Kevin sat on his rolling chair. He paused his video and minimized the video player. He wasn't going to masturbate in front of his brother after all.

Jacob asked, "Can I tell you something?"

"Just spit it out, little man. You know I'm not a snitch."

"Yeah..." Jacob whispered. He took a deep breath and nodded, mentally preparing himself for his confession. He said, "You... You were right. I want to... to kill. I never really thought about it, but I guess I've felt it for a long time. I'm just tired of being hated by everyone. I'm tired of everyone hating each other. Everything is so fucked up, it... it just makes me so mad. When I get angry, I feel like I hate everyone and everything. I don't know how to control these feelings anymore, Kev. I... I just... I want to kill."

Jacob paused to catch his breath and recompose himself. He still stared down at his lap, unable to make eye contact with his brother.

The young boy continued, "It's fucked up, man. Ever since I was a little kid in kindergarten, I knew life wasn't fair. It's *never* been fair to me. I always got bullied, I always got beat up, I always got left behind in class... It's not fair and I'm tired of it."

Kevin's eyes glowed with pleasure. He wasn't pleased by his brother's pain, he was simply delighted by his outlook on life. He finally broke through to him.

Kevin said, "That's good, Jacob. You see that? Now you're thinking like an adult. You're seeing the world for what it really is. So, you have a few options on the table. You can be like mom and all of these other idiots who follow the rules and live boring, miserable lives until they die... or you can do something with your hatred. You can have fun. You can live free. *You can kill.*"

Jacob had an urge to kill, images of murder constantly flashed in his mind, but he wasn't completely sold on the idea. Unlike his brother, his conscience was still alive and active. A demon sat on one of his shoulders and an angel sat on the other.

Jacob said, "I want to kill someone, but... I don't know how to explain it. I guess I just don't want to kill 'innocent' people, you know? I don't want to kill kids, moms, or dads. I don't want to hurt any animals, either. I can't do that."

Jacob stopped and thought about his own words. It was an interesting idea: some people could easily disregard violence against other people, but violence against animals was always unacceptable. Perhaps it was the natural innocence of an animal that inspired that mindset.

He gazed into his brother's eyes and said, "I don't want to kill homeless people, either. They never did anything wrong to me. I... I don't think they deserve it. I'm sorry if that makes you mad, but I won't do it."

Kevin smirked and said, "That's okay. It's alright. Listen, if we work together, we won't have to kill any homeless people. To be honest with you, I only killed homeless people because they were easy. It was getting boring, though. Anyway, we'll only kill 'bad' people, okay? Trust me when I say that. And, we're going to start with that pervert—*Sweets.* How does that sound? Hmm? Are you in?"

To Jacob, a thirteen-year-old boy with little real world experience, murdering bad people didn't seem wrong. He had witnessed vigilante justice in movies and in the news—and he liked it. He thought of himself as a crime fighter—a superhero without super powers. He thought: *pedophiles hurt kids, so why shouldn't I be allowed to hurt Dean?* From every angle, the idea made sense to him. He glanced over at Kevin and nodded—*I'm in.*

Kevin said, "Great. I knew you'd come around. Come on, let's talk about this. I've got a plan, but we won't be able to do anything until the weekend. I think mom will be over all of this drama by Friday, so we'll strike on Sunday." He glanced over at his bedroom door. He said, "Go lock the door, then come back here. We have a lot to talk about. For someone like this, our timing has to be perfect. No, no... *Everything* has to be perfect."

Jacob watched as Kevin opened a blank document on his computer. His brother apparently wanted to type out a plan for their first murder together. The younger sibling approached the door. He stared at the door knob, anxious. He wouldn't be able to turn back if he turned the lock.

Under his breath, he whispered, "I have to do this... They deserve it."

Jacob turned the lock and sealed his fate. He returned to his brother's side, ready to plan his first murder.

Chapter Eight

Sweets

The week came and went, each day filled with scheming. From Tuesday to Friday, the brothers walked to school together. And, before and after school, Jacob greeted Dean with a genuine smile. On Saturday, he even walked by the pedophile's house without a shirt—testing his resolve. He watered the seed of trust and built a relationship with him.

Sunday quickly arrived—a day for sleeping in, church, football, relaxation, and murder. At seven in the morning, the streets were quiet and desolate.

Jacob stood in front of Dean's chain-link fence, his backpack slung over his shoulder. He stared at the one-story house as he thought about the plan. He planned on killing Dean throughout the week, but uncertainty hit him at the last moment. Doubt clouded his mind, creating horrific scenarios that could lead to failure.

He took a deep breath, then he swiped the sweat from his brow, trying his best to look natural. He walked past the gate and strolled up the walkway, his legs wobbling with each step. His heart rate increased as he approached the door. He felt his heartbeat drumming through his entire body. He stopped in front of the door.

He whispered, "Just follow the plan."

Jacob knocked—*tap, tap, tap.* He glanced around

the neighborhood as he waited. The street was still empty. Thirty seconds passed and the door remained sealed. So, the teenager knocked again— *tap, tap, tap.* Then, a minute passed. That measly minute felt like an hour. The plan was crumbling before he even finished the first step.

Before the boy could run away, the sounds of locks *clicking* and *clacking* emerged. The door cracked an inch open.

Dean 'Sweets' Murray peeked through the gap, wearing a tattered tank top, striped boxers, and a pair of slippers. His eyes widened with confusion as he stared at Jacob. As a convicted sex offender, he didn't receive many visitors—excluding his parole officer's random visits. Yet, a boy willingly stood on his porch. *Am I still dreaming?*–he thought.

Dean stuttered, "He–Hey, kid. Wha–What do you... Um... What are you doing here?"

Jacob coughed to clear his throat, then he said, "Hey, Dean. I'm sorry for bothering you so early. I just... Well, I wanted to know if you could help me with my homework. I'm not doing so good in school, so I could use some help."

Dean rubbed the nape of his neck as he stared at Jacob with narrowed eyes, carefully analyzing his demeanor. He pulled the door open another inch, then he glanced over at the walkway. His parole officer was nowhere in sight, Jacob's mother wasn't hiding behind a tree or car—the coast was clear.

Baffled, Dean asked, "Why are you asking me?"

"I need help and... Well, no one else wants to help me. So, since you're so nice and chill, I thought you'd be able to help me out. You look smart, too. I mean, you're probably a lot smarter than me."

Dean sucked his lips inward and nodded. He wrestled with his inner-demons. The angel on his shoulder slumbered while the devil on his other shoulder whispered into his ear—*say 'yes,' do it.*

Noticing his reluctance, Jacob said, "I'll do anything if you help me with my algebra homework. I mean it, I'll do *anything* you want. Please, don't leave me like everyone else. *Please.*"

Dean bit his bottom lip. *Please*—Jacob's soft, innocent voice made his heart melt. He couldn't resist. He stared at Jacob's backpack, then he gazed into his eyes. The boy's request seemed genuine. He poked his head through the door and glanced around the neighborhood. The street was still empty, so there was no one around to see them.

He opened the door and said, "Okay. Come in, come in. Hurry."

Jacob nervously smiled and said, "Thanks."

As Jacob stepped into the house, Dean closed the door and secured the locks. The front door opened up to a dark hallway. There were four doors to the left. There was one door between two archways to the right. The first archway, directly to Jacob's right, led to the living room.

Dean walked into the living room and said, "Have a seat. I'll get you something to drink."

"Okay, thanks..."

Jacob shambled into the living room. He sat on the last seat of a three-seat sofa at the center of the room. He placed his backpack on the glass coffee table in front of the sofa, then he examined the area.

Bookshelves clung to the walls, brimming with old novels and obscure erotica. Some of the books didn't have titles on the spines, either. There was a recliner to the left and a fireplace to the right. A fire burned in the fireplace, crackling and popping. Directly ahead, through a wide archway spanning from wall-to-wall, he could see the kitchen over the bar.

Aside from lacking a television, the living room was normal. As a matter of fact, the entire house felt familiar. Jacob thought: *what was I expecting? Dead kids?* A loud *snapping* sound disrupted his thoughts.

Dean walked into the living room with an open can of Pepsi in his right hand. He placed the moist can on the coffee table next to the backpack. The sex offender sat on the middle seat of the sofa, directly beside Jacob. He smiled and scooted closer to him, then he tossed his arm over Jacob's shoulder—like a couple at a movie theater. To his utter surprise, Jacob didn't run away from him. *So far, so good,* he thought.

Dean said, "So, tell me about your homework, kid. What subject did you say it was? English? History? Or maybe it's, um... *physical education?*"

Jacob gazed into Dean's sparkling eyes. They had been neighbors for years, but he never noticed the look in his eyes—the look of pure evil. At that moment, he felt the pain of all of the pedophile's past victims. He had to keep his facade afloat, though. He took a deep breath, then he cracked a smile.

Jacob said, "I'm... I'm failing math. My teacher, Mr. Sullivan, said I'm probably going to get held back if I keep failing. So, you know, I thought maybe you could help me understand the homework, then I'd pass my tests."

Dean tilted his head and narrowed his eyes, as if he didn't trust him. He said, "I think you're lying."

Jacob shook his head and said, "No... No, I'm serious. I'm going to be held back if I don't pass. I–I need help. Like, I need *a lot* of help."

Dean didn't respond. He stared at the young teenager with a deadpan expression. Jacob stared back at Dean, trying to convince him with a pair of puppy eyes and a pouting lip. He was terrified, though. One wrong move could place him in harm's way.

Dean smirked and said, "Okay, okay."

He placed his hand on Jacob's knee, then he softly rubbed his thigh. Jacob shuddered uncontrollably. His touch was soft, but it still hurt him. He was being molested and he knew it. He couldn't say anything, though. He had to follow the plan. Fortunately, Dean misinterpreted Jacob's disgust for shyness so he didn't suspect a thing.

The pedophile said, "Well, in that case, I think I can help you out, kid. I'm not the best at math, but I'm sure I can teach you a thing or two. How hard can it be?"

Jacob loudly swallowed the lump in his throat, trying to stop himself from bursting into tears. He stuttered, "Th–Thanks. Should I... I don't know. Do I start with–"

Jacob stopped as Dean slowly moved his hand up his thigh. The pedophile gently squeezed the boy's leg, as if he were massaging him. Jacob trembled and stammered, but he couldn't muster the courage to scream or run. Molestation wasn't part of the plan, but it was happening before his very eyes. *What do I do? How do I buy time?*–he thought.

Dean stopped near the crotch of Jacob's jeans, the side of his hand scraping his zipper. He leered at the young boy, practically undressing him with his eyes. He wanted to fondle him, but it didn't seem romantic. He liked the boy after all. As a matter of fact, he started to believe that he *loved* him. He was easily enamored.

Dean pulled his hand away from Jacob's leg and said, "I don't want you to fail, Jacob. I want you to grow up to be big, strong, and successful. That's important to me. So, let's get started. Let me see your homework. I hope I remember most of this school junk."

Jacob sighed in relief. He glanced around the living room, as if he were searching for something. The hope in his eyes quickly turned into horror. He thought: *it should have happened by now.*

Dean asked, "Are you going to show me your homework or what?"

Thinking on his feet, Jacob asked, "Can I ask you a question first?"

"I guess so. What's up?"

"I just wanted to know, um... Why do they call you 'Sweets?' I heard that was your nickname before you moved here."

Dean chuckled, then he said, "It's amazing how stories follow us for so long... I'm no legend, but sometimes I feel like one. Sweets... They call me that because I love candy. Well, it wasn't just candy. I liked the sweet *things* in life." He caressed Jacob's cheek and said, "Sweet things, like you..."

Jacob clenched his jaw and stared down at himself—nervous, afraid, appalled. He couldn't say a word, though. Yet again, Dean believed the boy was simply bashful. He was aroused by his timid personality.

In a soft tone, Dean said, "You're so innocent, Jacob. It's really adorable. Listen, I know you're nervous, this might be your first time, but I want to make you feel a little more comfortable. I'm going to give you something sweet, okay?"

Eyes welling over with tears, Jacob stared down at his reflection on the coffee table. He listened as Dean leaned back in his seat and tugged on his boxers. He could *hear* the man groaning, he could *feel* him stroking himself. He knew Dean was masturbating beside him, but he didn't dare glance over at the pedophile. A single thought ran through his mind: *I'm fucked.*

As he shuffled on his seat, Dean patted Jacob's shoulder and said, "Come here, kid, suck on this. It'll give you something sweet. Come on, don't be–"

Clink—a metallic thudding sound echoed through the house. Dean fell forward and landed on the coffee table, twitching and groaning. Blood leaked from the back of his head. Droplets of blood dripped on the table—*plop, plop, plop.*

Jacob slowly turned and glanced over his shoulder, stunned. He couldn't help but smile upon spotting his brother. Kevin stood behind the sofa, holding an aluminum baseball bat in his gloved hands. His head was covered with a black ski mask.

Jacob whispered, "Finally..."

***

Dean coughed and grunted as he awoke. His vision was blurred by the blow to the head. The cut and the bump at the back of his dome stung. Parts of his body felt numb, but he still felt the blood and sweat streaming down the nape of his neck. He could hear the crackling flames in the fireplace, too, but the noise was muffled. His senses were distorted.

He thought: *what the hell did he do to me?*

He tightly closed his eyes and shook his head. He tried to stand up, but to no avail. He opened his eyes and stared down at himself. To his dismay, he was tied to a kitchen chair at regular intervals. His shins were tied to the chair's front legs, his arms were tied to the armrests, his thighs were tied to the seat, and his torso was tied to the backrest.

He glanced around, baffled. The coffee table was moved and he sat in front of the fireplace, only three meters away from the flames.

Dean tried to open his mouth to speak, but he was met with resistance. A thick strip of duct tape was placed over his mouth. His words and his whimpers were muffled. His eyes widened with fear as his vision slowly cleared. He spotted two figures standing in front of him. His worst nightmare came to fruition.

Jacob stood near the fireplace, visibly anxious. Kevin, still wearing his ski mask, paced back-and-forth in front of Dean.

Kevin said, "We went through this a million times: there's no turning back. If you had cold feet, you should have quit before you knocked."

"I... I'm just scared," Jacob responded, his voice cracking. "I don't know if we should do this."

"We should and we will. He has to be punished for his crimes. He has to die and we're going to kill him."

Upon hearing the plans of murder, Dean cried and screamed. His voice was muffled by the duct tape, but that didn't stop him from weeping. He even hopped in his seat, trying his best to break free from his restraints. The chair screeched on the hardwood floor with his fidgety movements. He wanted to explain his actions, he wanted to justify his crimes and beg for mercy, but he couldn't say a word.

Kevin glanced over at Dean and said, "It looks like the pedo is finally awake." He leaned closer to the pedophile and said, "I thought I killed you. Normally, I would be okay with that. Not today, though. Today is different. I'm going to teach my brother a few things. I hope you'll be patient with us."

Tears streaming down his cheeks, Dean indistinctly mumbled and shook his head. Of course, it didn't matter to the murderous siblings. Kevin huffed and rolled his eyes, amused by Dean's fear.

He pulled a pair of gloves out of the backpack. He handed the gloves to his younger brother.

Kevin said, "Alright, little man. Let's get started with some of the basics. We already started off on the wrong foot. Do you know why?"

As he put the gloves on, Jacob responded, "Because I wasn't wearing gloves before I started."

"*Exactly.* Whenever you commit a crime, even if it's not murder, you should be wearing gloves. You have to wear a ski mask, too. You don't want to make it easy for anyone who might be looking for you. I won't make you wear a mask now since this dumb bastard has already seen you. Remember that, though: *always* wear gloves and a mask during every crime."

"Yeah, I got it."

"Good. Don't forget it," Kevin responded. He ran his fingers through Jacob's feathery hair. He said, "We should cut your hair, too. We don't have to shave your head, we just have to trim it a little. You have to... to *limit* how much DNA you leave behind. Cops, detectives, the government... These people have technology that can link your ass hair back to you. It's like a fucking sci-fi movie. We have to be careful about that."

Ass hair—Jacob smiled upon hearing those words. The situation was serious, but the phrase was humorous. He couldn't help it. Kevin pulled two knives out of the backpack—a chef's knife and a boning knife. He handed the boning knife to his younger brother.

Dean whimpered and shuddered on the chair as

he spotted the weapons. *What the hell are they going to do to me?*–he thought.

Kevin said, "There are *a lot* of ways to kill a man. You can use your bare hands, but you need to be *really* strong for that. I don't recommend it. You can also use guns, but those are getting harder to find around here. And, even if you could find a gun, I don't recommend it. They're too loud."

Jacob asked, "What if you get a silencer?"

Kevin chuckled, then he said, "This isn't a movie. We're not in a video game. Silencers don't work like that in real life. They're still loud and they're still sloppy. Besides, guns are boring. A bullet to the head... It's just too easy." He wagged the knife at his brother and said, "Knives are my favorite. You can make a man squeal with a knife. You can stab a man a hundred times before someone else notices. You can't shoot a man a hundred times and get the same results. No, knives are special like that... They're not perfect, though. The more you stab, the more blood you have to deal with. Remember that."

Jacob stared down at his knife. He had seen the sharp blade in the kitchen before. It was nothing special. His brother made it sound like a weapon of mass destruction, though.

Kevin beckoned to Jacob and said, "Come here. I want you to stab this piece of shit."

Wide-eyed, Jacob glanced up at his brother and stuttered, "Wha–What? M–Me?"

"Yeah, *you*. Stab this bastard."

Jacob breathed heavily and slowly walked up to the chair, trembling like a nervous wreck. He stopped and gazed into Dean's eyes. To his disappointment, he couldn't see the evil in his eyes anymore. The man appeared confused and frightened. Despite his inappropriate actions, the pedophile looked innocent.

The conscience worked in mysterious ways.

Jacob stuttered, "I–I don't think I can do it. I'm... I'm sorry."

"You have to do it," Kevin responded. "I mean, what do you expect him to do if we let him live? You think he'll forget about this? You think he won't call the cops?"

"I just... I don't know how to do this, Kev. I'm fucking scared, man..."

"Well, let me help you."

Kevin grabbed Jacob's trembling wrist. He stared into his brother's eyes, communicating without uttering a word—*trust me*. Jacob was pushed to a corner. He didn't have any other options, so he nodded in agreement. Together, the brothers ran forward and thrust the blade into Dean's stomach.

Dean stared up at the ceiling and screamed, veins protruding from his neck and brow. His cheeks and ears reddened, his eyes bulged from his skull. The pain was excruciating, but he couldn't do anything to stop it. The brothers pulled the blade out. Blood stained the pedophile's tank top and dripped onto his boxers.

"Holy shit," Jacob whispered.

Kevin explained, "That was a good cut—*in*-and-*out*. If you stab someone in the stomach, it won't kill them instantly, but it will be very fucking painful.

Pain is good, especially if you have time to play. You can rip a man's stomach open, then play with his guts. You can see things your teachers won't show you in Health class. If you really want to make sure your victim dies, though, you should aim for the throat or the chest."

Jacob nodded in agreement as he digested the information. *The neck or the chest,* he thought, *it's that simple.*

Kevin grabbed Jacob's wrist and led the boning knife to Dean's neck. He ran the bloodied knife across the sex offender's neck, gliding the blade across his moist skin.

Kevin said, "If you cut his jugulars—these thick veins right here—he'll die in a few minutes. He'll bleed out like an animal in a slaughterhouse. I've done it before and... there was *so* much blood, you could take a bath in it. Your victim won't be able to scream, either. If you cut deep enough, he'll just gargle his own blood until he dies. It's amazing, isn't it?"

Dean breathed deeply through his nose as the blade sliced into his neck. The laceration was small, but it still stung. He was afraid the young man would accidentally slice into his jugular. Kevin's speech was terrifying. A droplet of blood dribbled from the small cut on his throat. The brothers pulled the knife away before they could cut his neck.

Kevin smirked and said, "But, people like this don't deserve to die so easily, Jacob. I mean, just look at him. We stabbed him, we held a knife to his throat, and he still popped a boner. He has a damn erection."

Jacob furrowed his brow as he stared at his brother. He glanced down at Dean's crotch, then he grimaced in disgust and turned away. Indeed, the pedophile was fully erect. His boxers protruded forward due to his erect penis—he was pitching a tent.

Dean shook his head and nervously smiled under the duct tape. The side of his mouth, his nose, and his left eye twitched. Rivers of sweat streamed across his face. He tried to speak, he wanted to explain his erection, but his words were muffled.

As Kevin reached for Dean's crotch, Jacob said, "Wait. What are you doing, man? That's dis–"

He stopped and turned away again. He stared at the crackling fireplace, anxious. Kevin moved Dean's boxers until his erect penis popped out of his fly, stiff like a pole. His loose scrotum also protruded from his boxers. He chuckled, amused by the pervert's deviance. He grabbed Jacob's shoulder and turned him around.

Jacob tried to pull away, but to no avail. He couldn't break his brother's grip. So, he stared up at the ceiling instead.

Kevin said, "This is what I've been talking about. This is a sick man. We beat him up, we tied him to a chair, and we stabbed him, but he still has a fucking boner! It's unbelievable, isn't it? I mean, he's hard because he *likes* it, Jacob. He probably feels a little guilty about it, but that guilt wouldn't have stopped him from fucking you if I weren't here. We have to fix him. This is what men like him deserve."

***

Jacob kept staring at the ceiling as he trembled like a child with a severe fever. He was overwhelmed by his fear and anxiety. He listened as Dean whimpered and wheezed.

Kevin riffled through the backpack, searching for the perfect tool to finish the job. He could have killed him with the chef's knife, but he wanted to set an example. Pedophiles had to be punished—and the consequences of that punishment had to be permanent. His eyes widened as he spotted the baseball bat on the floor beside his bag. *Perfect,* he thought.

He grabbed the baseball bat and stood up. He patted Jacob's shoulder and asked, "Would you like to do the honors?"

Eyes wide with fear, Jacob stared at the bat and stuttered, "Wha–What... What are we going to do?"

"We're going to make sure he never hurts a kid again. Do you want to do it?"

"N–No, I can't. I think I'll... I'll just watch, okay?"

"Okay, sure. Just make sure you're taking mental notes. I don't want you to forget this."

Dean squirmed and hopped on his chair as Kevin approached with the bat. Kevin rubbed the tip of the bat on Dean's scrotum and erect penis. The cold baseball bat and the ominous threat of violence didn't make his penis shrink, though. In fact, his cock pulsated and twitched with excitement. Fear aroused him.

Kevin held the bat with both hands. He stared down at Dean's genitals and lifted the bat over his head. He took a deep breath, then he swung down with all of his might. The bat struck his right testicle. Upon impact, Dean screamed and convulsed. The chair screeched on the floorboards.

Kevin beckoned to Jacob and said, "Get behind him and stop him from falling over."

Jacob, however, was paralyzed by his shock. His eyes and mouth were wide open as he stared at Dean's genitals. He could see his testicle twitching in his scrotum. *Did it explode?*–he thought.

Kevin barked, "Hurry!"

Jacob shook his head as he snapped out of his fear-induced trance. Legs like noodles, he staggered across the room and stopped behind the pedophile. He gripped the backrest of the chair and tightly closed his eyes.

Kevin lifted the bat over his head, then he struck down at Dean's genitals again. The barrel of the bat collided with the head of Dean's penis. The pedophile's erect penis was fractured with the blow, bent and crushed. Blood dripped from his urethra, streaming across his penis and scrotum, but that couldn't stop the teenager.

Kevin screamed as he struck him again. The bat hit his scrotum. His left testicle was ruptured upon impact. The edge of the bat also scraped his other testicle. His scrotum turned purple and blue, too.

Along with a copious amount of blood, semen spurted from his mangled penis. The excruciating pain caused him to experience an orgasm. It was simultaneously painful and euphoric—the ultimate orgasm. The gooey streams of cum landed on his boxers. Some of the semen even blended with the blood, creating a thick, pink fluid.

Dean involuntarily twitched and thrust his hips. He breathed deeply through his nose as he stared down at his bloody crotch, his eyelids flickering erratically.

Kevin sneered in disgust as he stared at the bleeding penis. He said, "Look at yourself... You cummed after I beat your dick and balls with a bat. What the hell is wrong with you? Fucking pervert..." He turned his attention to Jacob and said, "We're not done with him yet. Pull the tape off of his mouth."

Jacob was rendered speechless by the barbaric act of violence. The makeshift castration was jarring. It wasn't part of the plan. His stomach twisted and turned. He felt as if vomit were clogged in his throat. *How could he do something like this?*– he thought.

Kevin shouted, "Jacob! Listen to me, little man. I want you to pull the tape off of his mouth. When I tell you to, I want you to put it back. Okay?"

Jacob couldn't utter a word. He responded with a reluctant nod—*okay.* From left-to-right, he pulled on the tape. The tape remained attached to Dean's face.

As the pedophile gasped for air, Kevin pulled a pair of pliers out of his back pocket. He closed the jaws of the pliers over Dean's rotten canine tooth, then he pulled back. The tooth, despite its rotten core, was resilient. So, he wiggled the pliers and loosened it, then he tugged on the tooth again. With the second tug, the tooth slid out and slimy blood dripped from his gums.

Dean screamed, "Oh, fuck! You sick son of a bitch! Oh, God, why–"

"Put it back on," Kevin interrupted. Jacob trembled and glanced around, reluctant. Kevin sternly said, "*Now.*"

Jacob cried as he covered Dean's mouth with the tape. He stepped in reverse until the back of his legs collided with the coffee table. Dean's head swayed left-and-right, as if he were dazed by a powerful punch. He coughed and grunted as he trembled in his seat. His chest and stomach constantly inflated and deflated. The pain was insufferable.

Kevin shoved the tooth into his pocket. He grabbed the knife and said, "Remember: always aim for the jugular."

Without saying another word, he thrust the knife into Dean's neck. The blade penetrated his bulging jugular. He pulled the knife out and stepped back. He watched as blood spewed from the sex offender's neck. The blood streamed down his neck and drenched his shirt. He turned his attention to his victim's eyes. He couldn't help but smile— Dean's eyes had rolled to the back of his head.

Kevin said, "He'll be dead in a minute or two. It's time to pack up."

He knelt down in front of the backpack. He grabbed a towel from the bag, then he wiped his arms and neck. He wore black from head-to-toe, so he wasn't concerned with the blood on his clothing. After cleaning himself, he used the same towel to wipe the blood off of the knife and bat. He didn't have to wipe any other fingerprints since both of the siblings wore gloves.

Awed, Jacob walked around the chair with his eyes locked on Dean. He analyzed every twitch on the pedophile's body, he memorized the look of death on his face. The sight was haunting. Guilt ate away at his heart, devouring his innocence.

As he shoved the tools into his backpack, Kevin said, "Come here, Jacob. It's time to go." Jacob couldn't move. Kevin stood up and shouted, "Hey! It's time to go! Come here!"

Tears streamed down Jacob's cheeks as he closed his eyes. Swiping at his face with each step, he shambled towards his brother with his head down. He didn't want his brother to see his tears. *What kind of person would cry for a pedophile?*

Jacob stuttered, "O–Okay. I'm... I'm ready to go."

Kevin carefully examined every inch of his brother's body. He searched for the smallest speck of blood. To his utter surprise, Jacob was clean.

Kevin said, "You look good, little man. You're clean, you're safe. You're going to be fine, just don't touch anything. Come on, let's go."

Kevin ran into the kitchen and headed to the back door. Without glancing back at their victim, Jacob followed his brother and escaped from the scene of the crime.

Chapter Nine

Advice

Kevin and Jacob walked up the walkway and approached their house. Kevin casually strolled up to the front door, unperturbed by his actions. Jacob constantly glanced over his shoulder, anxious and frightened. The siblings were relieved to see their mother wasn't home yet. They had time to plan their next move.

As soon as Jacob entered the house, Kevin closed the door and turned the locks. He glanced over at his brother with a steady expression, then he smirked.

Kevin said, "We did it. We fucking did it, man!"

Jacob stared down at his sneakers and said, "You did all of the dirty work."

"That's true, but you definitely helped. I mean, if it wasn't for you, I could have never killed that bastard. It took a little longer than I thought, but it's not like we're trying to break any records. No, no. It was... It was perfect, Jacob."

Jacob pulled his cell phone out of his pocket and checked the time. To his utter surprise, it was nearly ten in the morning. He spent close to three hours baiting, torturing, and murdering the pedophile. The Sunday morning—which he usually spent watching TV or playing video games—was used for murder. It was a difficult fact to swallow.

88

Kevin said, "I know you probably feel strange right now. I felt the same way after my first kill. I want you to know: *it's okay*. You did something good today. *We* did good today. We got rid of a monster— a *real* monster." He patted Jacob's shoulder and said, "It takes a while to get used to it, but it'll grow on you. You should get some rest. Take a nap, play some video games, relax. I'll take care of everything else, okay?"

Jacob nodded and said, "Okay."

Jacob withdrew to his bedroom. He lay in bed with his fingers interlocked over his stomach, blankly staring at the ceiling. A minute quickly turned into an hour, an hour turned into two, and so on. The sun rose to its zenith, blessing the city with a welcomed warmth, then it fell beyond the horizon.

His mother arrived in the afternoon, tired and frustrated. She noticed Jacob's unusual isolation, but Kevin covered for him. He claimed his little brother was sick, blaming it on spoiled milk, and she believed him. That was how it worked in the White household.

As soon as nighttime arrived, a man's faint voice meandered through the house. Like a teenage girl with strict parents, Isabel smuggled another lover into her home. The couple rushed into the master bedroom and the lovemaking started. Thumping and moaning echoed through the house—the soundtrack of sex.

At an hour before midnight, Jacob let out a deep sigh. He couldn't sleep. The sex didn't bother him. The stray cat meowing outside of his bedroom window didn't disturb him. His mind was flooded with thoughts of Dean's murder. A medley of conflicting emotions flowed through his body— anger, disgust, sadness, fear, *excitement.*

At heart, he actually enjoyed killing Dean. He was afraid to admit it, though. His actions made him feel vile and wicked. His conscience was still alive.

Jacob whispered, "I have to talk to someone. I have to... I have to do something about this."

He stood from his seat and walked out of his room. He opened Kevin's door and stood in the doorway. As expected, his older brother was nowhere in sight. Another pornographic video played on the monitor. It was a video of a mature woman fucking a younger man. The scenario seemed eerily familiar.

Jacob stared at the closet door. The pieces were easy to connect. *He's always in the closet,* he thought, *but why?*

He took a deep breath, then he tiptoed into the bedroom. He quietly approached the closet door. He could hear a *squelching* sound in the closet. His curiosity got the best of him. He pulled the door open with one swift movement, then he gasped and stepped back. He was shocked by his discovery.

Kevin squatted under his coats and shirts, his boxers wrapped around his ankles as he vigorously masturbated. He smiled as he glanced over at his brother. It was the type of smile that jokingly said: *oops, you caught me.*

Before Jacob could say a word, Kevin lifted his boxers up to his waist and held his index finger over his mouth—*shush.* Fortunately for him, Jacob was speechless.

Kevin walked out of his closet and whispered, "Keep your voice down. I don't want them to hear us."

"Them?" Jacob repeated in an uncertain tone.

Kevin stepped aside, pointed into his closet, and said, "*Them.*"

Jacob spotted a small circle of illumination pouring into the dark closet. There was a waist-high hole on the wall behind the clothing. He crouched down and peered through the hole.

In a soft whisper, he stuttered, "Wha–What the fuck?"

Through the hole, he could see into his mother's closet. Since his mother always left her closet open, he could also see into her bedroom. Although the room was dark, solely illuminated by the light from the television, he had the perfect view of her queen-sized bed. His mother, nude and sweaty, jumped on the mattress. A nude man joined her. The couple giggled as they kissed.

Jacob staggered away from the door, shaking his head in disbelief. The truth dawned onto him: his older brother enjoyed watching his mother's sexual escapades.

Kevin patted Jacob's shoulder and said, "Hey, little man, if you want, I can give you a few minutes alone in my closet. I won't tell anyone, I promise."

Jacob stared at his brother with wide eyes. He was flabbergasted by his offer. The thought of watching his mother with a stranger never crossed his mind. He caught a glimpse of the porn on the monitor. At that moment, he realized it was incest porn—fake, poorly-acted incest porn.

He shook his head and stuttered, "N–No. I... I don't want to."

"Why? Are you too good for our mom? Do you think it's creepy or something? Do you think *I'm* creepy? Is that it?"

"No. I just... I don't want to do this."

Kevin smirked and said, "Well, you're going to do it and you're going to like it."

"Wha–What? I said–"

Mid-sentence, Kevin shoved Jacob into his closet, then he closed the door. He leaned on the door and laughed. The coats and shirts hanging from the pole stopped Jacob from falling to the floor. He rushed forward and tackled the door, but to no avail. He couldn't overpower his older brother.

Before Jacob could hit the door and scream, Kevin said, "Keep it down in there. If mom hears you, she'll come in here and catch you. You don't want her to catch you, do you? Do you know how embarrassing that would be? I wouldn't be able to show my face in this house if she caught me. You have to stay quiet."

Jacob slowly lowered his arms and stepped back. His brother was right. If he caused a scene, his mother would barge into the room and catch him.

In a soft tone, Kevin said, "There's nothing wrong with taking a peek, Jacob. Just pretend like it's someone else's mom. Go on, check it out."

Jacob glanced over his shoulder and stared at the

hole on the wall. His mother's tender moaning seeped into the closet and danced into his ears. The sound of sex called to him, sending him an invitation he couldn't refuse. He heard his mother's voice in his head. The voice said: *come and watch me, sweetie, it's natural.* He crouched under the coats and peeked through the hole.

Isabel and the mysterious man had sex in the cowgirl position. She rode his cock, bouncing up-and-down, and he thrust upward into her. His mother's ass and the man's scrotum jiggled with each thrust. The headboard *thumped* on the wall and the bed frame *screeched* on the hardwood floor. It looked and sounded like a scene from a pornographic video.

Jacob stared down at his crotch and smiled. He wasn't aroused by his mother's sex. He was curious, he wanted to know more about sex, but he wasn't titillated by his mother's figure. He sighed in relief. *Maybe I'm not like him,* he thought, *maybe I'm actually normal.* He already helped his brother commit a murder, but he wasn't completely deviant —that fact brought some clarity to his mind.

Jacob gently knocked on the closet door and whispered, "I'm ready to come out. I'm... I don't want to be in here. I mean, I don't care about this, I just don't want to be here. I just wanted to talk to you. Can we talk, Kev?"

Kevin stared at the porn on his monitor as he leaned back on the door with his arms crossed. He was disappointed in his brother's lackluster reaction. He expected him to masturbate to their mother, then he expected a show of gratitude. Instead, his brother showed his true colors—a cowardly conformist.

He opened the door and said, "Sure, sure. Go ahead and sit down."

Jacob walked out of the closet, relieved. He sat on the bed with his hands on his knees, keeping his eyes on his brother. Kevin sat down on the rolling chair. He closed his video player, then he glanced over at Jacob.

The killer smiled and asked, "So, what do you want to talk about?"

"I wanted to talk about this morning."

"Yeah? What about it? I offered to make you breakfast, didn't I? It's not my fault you weren't hungry."

"That's not it. I'm... I'm talking about the... the murder. I know you said we were doing the right thing and I know Sweets was a bad person, but I still feel... *bad*."

Kevin said, "We've been through this. You just need some time to adjust. I felt the same way after my first kill, but I was feeling better by the next day. It's normal. Listen, your 'conscience' is going to go away soon. All of that right and wrong bullshit the government brainwashed you with... It's going to be gone. That's when the real fun is going to start."

Jacob responded, "I'm not sure about that."

"What? Why? What's the matter?"

"I don't know how to explain it. I wanted to kill Dean, but I don't think I liked doing it. Maybe I'm not a killer. Maybe I'm just a thinker."

"*No.* Don't talk like that, little man. Deep down, we're all killers. There's a killer in mom, there's a killer in that guy she's fucking, and there's a killer in our neighbor. Most people bury their killers so that they never kill anyone themselves. Sometimes, the killer breaks free from his grave and goes on a rampage. People like us... We embrace our inner killers. We can control ourselves as long as we keep killing at a good pace."

Jacob didn't know how to respond to his brother's passionate speech. Yet, he found himself agreeing with Kevin's main point. He believed everyone harbored homicidal tendencies—some people were just better at controlling themselves.

Kevin said, "We should go out to the No-Light District. I want to show you something."

As Kevin stood up and approached the closet, Jacob responded, "Now? *At night?*"

As he slipped into his jeans, Kevin said, "Yeah. I want to show you around. There's a lot of fucked up shit at the No-Light District. When we get there, you'll see how fucked up the world is." He tossed a shirt over his head, then he slipped into his coat. He continued, "Besides, I want to spend time with you. You're my little brother and I want to make sure we stay close."

Jacob asked, "What about mom? What if she catches us?"

"She won't. She'll fuck that guy for a few more hours, she'll kick him out, then she'll sleep until six or seven. She won't notice a thing. Just go get dressed. I'll meet you in the living room in five minutes."

Jacob glanced over at the closet and thought about his mother. He could still hear her moaning. *I don't have anything better to do,* he thought.

As Jacob walked across the room, Kevin said, "Don't forget your gloves. I don't want you to catch anything out there."

Kevin watched as his brother exited the room. He put on his gloves, then he grabbed two ski masks and a lighter from his dresser. He shoved the supplies into his back pockets so his brother wouldn't see them. He knelt down and pulled a machete out from under the dresser. A torn white t-shirt was wrapped around the twelve-inch blade.

With the cloth still wrapped around the blade, he shoved the machete into his waistband. With that, he was ready for a night on the town.

Chapter Ten

The No-Light District

"This is it," Kevin said as he slowed his jog to a stroll.

Jacob stopped behind him and breathed noisily, his hands on the small of his back as he struggled to catch his breath. He glanced around the area. He had been there before, but never by himself—or at night. He only ever saw the dilapidated area from the safety of the backseat of his mother's car. During the cold night, a malevolent aura swept through the area.

The siblings found themselves in the Red-Light District, which was also known as the *No-Light District* due to the lack of electricity in the area.

They were surrounded by dozens of abandoned apartment buildings. There were a few deserted ground-level stores, too. All of the buildings were dilapidated and vandalized, burdened with broken windows and decorated with vibrant graffiti. The streets were swamped with trash—food wrappers, empty bottles, broken glass, plastic bags, and bodily fluids.

As he jogged across the street, Kevin beckoned to Jacob and shouted, "Come on! It's over here!"

Jacob glanced over at his brother and sighed. He reluctantly followed Kevin's lead. He furrowed his brow as he spotted their destination—an abandoned department store.

As they ran across the parking lot, Jacob asked, "What is this place?"

Without stopping, Kevin responded, "It used to be a K-Mart or something. They changed it, though."

"*They?*" Jacob repeated, confused.

"You'll see."

Kevin pushed the doors open and proudly walked into the large store, acting as if he owned the place. Jacob stopped in the doorway, awed.

As Kevin explained, the department store's interior was different. The store was converted into a homeless encampment. The homeless built shanties inside of the store. The homemade shacks were made of corrugated metal, plywood, and even cardboard. Like street lamps, fires burned in trash cans at regular intervals. Small pathways were created between the shanties, acting as improvised roads.

Most of the homeless inhabitants slept in their makeshift homes. A few of the transients settled around the burning trash cans, searching for warmth or cooking a late-night snack. There were some troublemakers—bickering and wrestling—in the area, too. It looked as if there were a small city inside of the building.

Again, Kevin beckoned to Jacob and said, "Follow me and stay close."

Jacob was an open-minded teenager, he wasn't prejudice or hateful, but he didn't feel safe in the department store. He was a child surrounded by a group of strangers after all. So, he jogged forward and stayed close to his brother.

As he walked, Kevin said, "Look at these people, Jacob. What do you see?"

Jacob glanced around the indoor shanty town. He saw a wide range of homeless people. Some of the homeless people slept while others ate, drank, and chattered. A few of them had sex, too. All types of sex seemed common in the shanty town. Some of the homeless people even treated themselves to their favorite street drugs—black tar heroin and cocaine. The addicts wrestled and argued about the drugs, too.

Jacob responded, "I see people."

"Exactly," Kevin said. "These are people who have been pushed away from 'mainstream' society, so they don't follow modern society's norms. So, they're people in their purest form. What are these people doing?"

"They're.... They're living."

"Yes, Jacob, but what are they *doing?*"

"I–I don't know. I guess they're–"

Kevin stopped and turned towards his brother. He said, "I'll tell you what they're doing. These people are doing drugs. They're fucking like animals. They're fighting each other. They're living in hell. These people... They've given up on life."

Jacob shook his head. Kevin's speech was cynical. He spoke solely about the negative aspects of the shanty town while conveniently ignoring the positives. Even in the darkest, most desolate pits of mankind, there was always a glimmer of hope.

Jacob said, "Kev, some of these people are like us.

They don't live in a house like us, but they're just trying to live. They're talking, they're eating, they're sleeping. These are normal people."

Kevin nodded and responded, "Yeah, I guess that's true. I just brought you hear to, um... What's the word I'm looking for? I wanted to... to... to *demonstrate* one of the world's problems. These poor people are teaching us about hypocrisy."

Jacob nervously smiled and shook his head. His befuddled reaction said: *what?!* His brother was going off on another tangent. He couldn't keep up.

Kevin said, "Don't look at me like that. Just listen, okay? People are always talking about helping the homeless, right? Every day, some rich bastard gets on the news and scolds us 'normal' people because we don't do enough. We didn't go vote, we didn't raise a billion fucking dollars for a charity, *we didn't do our part.* But, in reality, no one ever does anything about it—*no one.* Liberal celebrities— some who are worth *hundreds* of *millions* of dollars —ask for higher taxes to help the poor while using fucking loopholes so they don't pay taxes on their mansions! These, um, conservatives are no better, little man. They talk about bringing jobs to the poor so that they're not-so-poor, but they never get those jobs. It's all bullshit. All of it is *political* bullshit!"

He paused to catch his breath. A fire burned in his livid eyes, adrenaline pumped through his veins. He glared at a group of homeless men to his right. The men watched him with furrowed brows. The murderous teenager smiled and waved—*nothing to see here.*

He turned towards his brother and said, "Fake humanitarians, pseudo-liberals, all-talk-no-action politicians... They make people feel bad for allowing *this* to happen without doing anything about it. Well, let me tell you something, Jacob. I've come to realize that we shouldn't feel bad. I realized that the government—that machine—has been using guilt to control us. It doesn't work that way, though. I'm too smart. I'm too enlightened. If everyone else is inhumane, hiding behind self-righteousness like a bunch of cowards, why shouldn't we just embrace it? There is no humanity without *in*-humanity, right? So, why shouldn't we be 'inhumane?' Why can't we be 'bad?' The truth is: everyone wants to be inhumane, everyone wants to be a killer, but they're just too afraid to do it. When we kill, Jacob, we're just doing what everyone else wishes they could do... We're being free."

What the hell are you talking about?—Jacob had to stop himself from uttering that question. He was listening to the ramblings of a madman. Some of it made sense, but most of it sounded like nonsense. Homeless people, liberals, conservatives, hypocrisy —he struggled to find the connection. His brother sounded like a psychopathic conspiracy theorist.

Yet, the ending of the speech resonated with him. He thought: *everyone wants to kill, they're just too afraid to do it.*

Before Jacob could utter a word, a woman limped towards the boys. The brothers stared at her with raised brows.

The woman was obviously homeless. They were

in a homeless encampment after all. There were gray streaks across her filthy blonde hair. She had wrinkles on her droopy face. Her blue eyes were listless, dull and hopeless. She was missing a few teeth, but she still tried to smile. She wore a tattered coat over a dirty tank top, short-shorts, and sneakers.

The woman smirked and said, "Hey, boys. I haven't seen y'all 'round here before. Y'all looking for some company?" The siblings continued to stare at her with steady expressions. The woman said, "Five for a blowjob, ten for the works. Since there's two of y'all, we double the price. Deal?"

Although he lived on the poor side of town, Jacob lived a sheltered life. So, he had never met a prostitute before. He expected someone cleaner and sexier, like the women he saw on porn sites. Judging from her constant twitching and scratching, the woman appeared to be a desperate drug addict looking for a quick buck.

Kevin asked, "Can I throat-fuck you?" Jacob glanced over at his brother with wide eyes. Kevin walked around the prostitute and asked, "Can I *skull*-fuck you? Do you like anal? Huh? Can I bite on your nipples? Can I chew on your clit?"

The woman rubbed her shoulders, as if she were frightened. She was just scratching herself, though. *Itchy blood*—it was a side-effect of her addiction to heroin.

The prostitute said, "You can do *anything* you want to me as long as you got the money. You got money, don't you? Or, do... do you got some tar?"

Kevin stopped in front of the woman. He glared into her forlorn eyes. He huffed, then he kicked her knee in. As her bones broke through her skin, protruding from the back of her leg, the woman howled in pain and fell to the floor. Jacob gasped and winced upon hearing the unnerving *popping* sound from her broken leg.

Through her gritted teeth, the woman hissed, "You bastard! You little... Fuck!"

Kevin walked over the prostitute, his fists clenched. His entire body moved with each heavy breath. He was inexplicably angry. He bent over, then he punched down at the woman's face. He hit her with a barrage of hooks—left, right, left, *right.* He grabbed a fistful of her hair and lifted her head, then he kicked the side of her dome with all of his might. The kick knocked her unconscious.

He released his grip on her hair, causing the back of her head to collide with the hard ground. He wasn't done, though. He started stomping on her face. Her nose was broken, her lips were lacerated, and a handful of her remaining teeth were displaced. Blood covered every inch of her face. Blood and saliva foamed out of her mouth.

Jacob watched the brutal beating in utter awe. He glanced over at the other homeless people. To his utter surprise, they didn't seem to care. They kept to themselves.

Jacob pushed his brother and shouted, "Stop it, man! You're going to kill her!"

Kevin lifted his hands up to his chest and nodded, as if to say: *okay, okay, I'm done.* He walked around the woman's unconscious body, trying to catch his breath.

He said, "I'm... I'm done here. I made my point. Let's go outside. I need... I need some fresh air. It smells like shit in here."

Jacob, awed by the attack, stood in silence. He stared down at the unconscious prostitute, then over at his brother, then over at the other homeless people. Everyone acted as if nothing had happened. He felt bad for the woman, but he couldn't do anything about it. He certainly couldn't comfort her without having to call an ambulance. *If they don't care about their own, why should I?*–he thought.

He jogged away from the scene of the crime and followed his brother out of the homeless encampment.

The siblings walked to the side of the abandoned building. They sat on the floor beside and overflowing dumpster. The smell was still atrocious, but it was easier to breathe outside. There was a pinch of fresh air in each breath.

As he vacantly stared at the floor, Jacob asked, "What happened in there? Why did you do... *that* to her?"

Kevin flicked a pebble with his thumb and watched it roll. He said, "I'm sorry about that, Jacob. I lost myself. These people... I don't know, I just always feel like they're asking for it. She just walked up to us and interrupted my lesson like... like... like if I didn't even matter. It pissed me off. I lost my cool. Forgive me?"

Jacob examined his brother with a set of

narrowed eyes. He thought about his brother's apology. It seemed honest, but he didn't appear remorseful. He couldn't challenge him about it, either. That would only lead to a fight he would surely lose. He decided to bury the hatchet and forget about the bloody confrontation.

He said, "Yeah, I forgive you..."

Jacob glanced over his shoulder and stared at the wall behind him. He thought about the prostitute— *before* the beating. He wasn't attracted to the woman, but, like most teenagers, he was interested in sex.

He coughed to clear his throat, then he said, "Hey, Kev, um... What is... What is sex like? I mean, have you done it before?"

Kevin chuckled, then he said, "Of course. It's hard to explain everything, but... it feels great. Loose or tight, I can never tell the difference. It *always* feels good to me. Damn, now that you mention it, I feel like fucking something now..."

Jacob asked, "So, you've really done it before?"

"I've done it a lot. When you're free, when you stop believing in good and bad, you can do anything you want. That feeling, the feeling of freedom... It's almost as good as sex."

Jacob gazed at his brother with inquisitive eyes. One question ran through his mind: *have you ever raped someone?* His brother's vague explanation hinted at a crime. Yet again, he couldn't confront him about it. False rape accusations could destroy a person's life.

Jacob said, "I wish I could try it."

Kevin responded, "Well, you *should* try it. You're missing out, little man." He glanced over at his brother and asked, "Why didn't you jack off in the closet?"

"Wha–What?"

"I know you looked through the peephole in my closet. Why didn't you jack off to mom?"

"Because she's our mom. It's wrong."

"Shit, man. You're still with that? After everything I've said to you? Get it through your head, Jacob. Stop thinking about right and wrong. There's no such thing in this world. It's all fake. Okay? You can masturbate to mom if you want to. Hell, you could fuck her if you wanted to... and it would probably feel really good."

Jacob grimaced and shook his head, disgusted. Yet, a deviant thought crept into his mind: *what would it feel like to have sex with my mom?* He thought about the people around the world who participated in incestuous relationships. He didn't think it was common, but he knew it happened. In fact, at that very moment, someone—*somewhere*—was having sex with a relative.

Upon spotting a stray Beagle dog in the parking lot, Kevin said, "If you don't want to fuck mom, you could always fuck an animal. Trust me, it feels the same."

Jacob sneered in disgust and asked, "How the hell do you know that?"

"I've done it before. I fucked a golden retriever. It was some of the best sex I ever had. I had that bitch howling for hours."

"You... You're fucking sick, man."

"I know, I know. I'm horny, too. I think I'm going to have to fuck this dog right here."

"*What?*"

Kevin staggered to his feet. He chuckled as he approached the stray dog. He glanced back at his brother as he pulled his zipper down.

Jacob stood up and said, "Don't do it. Please, Kev, this is too much."

"Too much? I'm just going to fuck it, Jacob. Sex is natural, remember? This sweet dog might even enjoy it."

Teary-eyed, Jacob clasped his hands in front of his chest and said, "I'm begging you. Don't do this. I– I can't watch this. I'll never forgive you if you–"

Jacob stopped and furrowed his brow as his brother burst into a guffaw. Kevin pulled his zipper up and approached his brother.

The psychopathic teenager said, "I'm sorry. I was just messing with you. I'm not *that* sick, little man." Jacob forced a smile—*it was just a sick joke.* Kevin patted his brother's shoulder and said, "Come on, let's go."

"Home?"

"No. I want to show you something else. Here, put this on."

Kevin pulled two ski masks out of his back pocket. He handed one to Jacob, then he tossed the other one over his head.

Kevin said, "Follow me."

Jacob was awed by his brother's audacity. He wasn't the brightest student, but he wasn't blind, either. The masks meant his brother was planning something illegal. He couldn't leave without him, though. It wasn't safe. He put on the mask, then he reluctantly followed Kevin's lead.

Chapter Eleven

The Wolf

The brothers approached an abandoned apartment building across the street from the department store. Like the other buildings, the three-story structure was dilapidated and vandalized. The broken windows were boarded with plywood. The doors were removed from the doorways. The walls were tagged with gang graffiti and dappled with bird shit. A few people could be heard coughing, groaning, and arguing inside of the building.

Kevin and Jacob stood in the main entrance of the apartment building. The siblings stared into a dark, grimy hallway. The floor was flooded with garbage—tin cans, old newspapers, used condoms, hazardous syringes, and even feces. The paint on the walls was chipped and replaced with spray paint. There were three doors to the left and two doors to the right. To the right, a staircase also led to the other floors of the building.

As Kevin strolled into the building, Jacob whispered, "What is this place, Kev? What are you going to do?"

Disregarding the questions, Kevin said, "Watch your step. There's shit everywhere in this place. Watch out for the ceiling, too. This old building could fall on us at any moment."

His feet firmly planted in the doorway, Jacob

leaned into the corridor and glanced around. He didn't see anyone in the dark hallway. He heard a pair of dull footsteps and muffled voices upstairs, though. A malevolent aura lingered in the building. He couldn't help but wonder if ghosts inhabited the apartments.

Standing in the doorway of the first apartment to the right, Kevin beckoned to Jacob and whispered, "Over here."

Jacob couldn't control his curiosity. *What is he hiding in there? What does he want to show me this time?*–he thought. He took a deep breath, then he walked into the building. He lunged over the stale feces and broken syringes until he reached his brother's side. Like a dog listening to a strange noise, he cocked his head to the side as he stared into the apartment's living room.

In the living room, next to a pile of used syringes, a grizzled homeless man slept on a bed comprised of flattened cardboard boxes. His sooty lips fluttered with each snore. His unkempt beard— black, gray, and dirty—protruded every which way. He wore layers upon layers of tattered coats, ripped jeans, and scuffed boots.

Kevin leaned on the wall beside the door. He slid down to his ass, his eyes locked on the slumbering homeless man. Jacob crept into the room, his heels and shoulders raised. He didn't have any other options, so he sat down beside his brother.

Kevin whispered, "I've been watching this guy for a while. Like all of the other hobos in this area, he has no family and no one cares about him—*no one.*

He... he's perfect." He glanced over at his brother and asked, "Are you ready to kill?"

Awed, Jacob repeated, "*Kill?*" He shook his head and said, "No, man. I... I thought we just came over here to hang out."

"We are hanging out. And, now I want to kill."

"Kevin, I thought we were only going to kill bad people. I told you: I don't want to hurt animals and I don't want to kill homeless people. You promised."

Kevin responded, "Just because he's homeless that doesn't mean he's not 'bad.' When you think about it, most people end up being homeless because they *are* bad. They get into fights, they do drugs, and they spend their money like idiots... They make bad choices so they're 'bad' people, right? Isn't that how it works in your little world?"

Jacob rebutted, "That's not true. They're normal people. You know that."

"Whatever. It doesn't matter. I know this one is bad. Like I said, I've been watching him. He's a junkie. He robs and hurts innocent people. He takes their stuff, he trades their shit for drugs, he gets high, then he repeats the process—over and over and over. I've seen him rape someone, too. He raped another homeless woman. She was so fucked up on drugs, she didn't even feel it. But, *I* saw it. He deserves to die."

Jacob didn't believe his brother. The story was too convenient. Kevin painted the homeless man as a monster, but he didn't have any proof. Considering his history of violence and manipulation, he simply wasn't trustworthy.

Jacob responded, "I'm not killing an innocent person."

"He's *not* innocent," Kevin snapped.

The siblings glared at each other, infuriated. Jacob was anxious and frightened, but he refused to back down from the confrontation. Kevin was simultaneously angry and proud, surprised by his little brother's sudden surge of confidence.

Jacob said, "If you try to do anything to him, I'll... I'll go home."

Kevin huffed, then he said, "You're not going to walk home alone. You might think you're tough right now, but that won't last when you walk out there by yourself. You don't believe me about this guy, I can see it in your eyes, but, deep down, you're afraid one of these other guys out here will grab you and *rape you.* Don't lie to yourself, Jacob. Don't hide your true self like those cowards on TV. If one of 'em is bad, then they're all bad. If they're all bad, then who cares if we kill this one?"

Jacob saw the evil in Kevin's eyes, but he couldn't do anything to stop him. He didn't agree with his brother's assessment, either. Yet, he knew Kevin was correct about one thing: he couldn't walk home alone. Despite claiming most of them were good, he was afraid of walking home alone because he didn't trust all of the homeless people in the area. Just as Kevin explained, he was a hypocrite.

Jacob thought: *they're good people, aren't they? Why would I say that if I didn't believe it? Is Kevin right? Was I just brainwashed into believing it?*

Kevin stood up and said, "I won't force you to kill

tonight, Jacob. You don't even have to get your hands dirty. I... I have to do this, though. I can't control myself. If I don't do something, if I don't kill him, I'm afraid I might hurt someone close to us. I might hurt your little girlfriend, Molly. I might hurt that sweet old lady that lives down the street from us. I might even hurt our own mom. I don't want to do *that,* so I have to do *this.* Just... Just close your eyes and wait until this is over. It'll only take a few minutes."

Jacob sniffled and lowered his head, horrified. His brother's threats of violence were worrisome. He couldn't risk his mother's safety, he couldn't put Molly in danger's way. He closed his eyes and nodded—*go ahead.* Although his eyes were closed, Jacob could hear the entire confrontation.

Kevin kicked the homeless man's leg and shouted, "Wake up, old man! I want to play a game. Get up!"

The homeless man turned on his makeshift bed and glanced up at Kevin. He shook his head and mumbled indistinctly, frustrated by the rude awakening, then he turned over on his bed.

Kevin barked, "Wake up!"

Drowsy, the man responded, "Get away from me, boy. This is my spot."

"I don't give a fuck. Get up or die."

"What... What did you say to me? You dumb... bastard. I told you already: this is my spot! Get away from me before you get yourself hurt. Dumb motherfucker..."

"I don't have time for this."

Jacob opened his eyes to a squint. He watched as Kevin pulled the machete out of his pants. He closed his eyes and shook his head. He thought: *he tricked me, he always planned on doing this.* He winced upon hearing a moist *thudding* sound. To his dismay, he recognized the sound. It was the sound of a machete chopping at something—*or someone.*

The sound of a struggle followed the noise. He heard footsteps, shuffling, grunting, and groaning. Kevin and the homeless man even muttered obscenities at each other—bastard, bitch, cocksucker, cunt, fucker. The men clearly wrestled in the living room. Another *thud* echoed through the room, then someone gasped and croaked.

Jacob opened one eye, curious. His eye widened with fear upon spotting the blood leaking out of the homeless man's throat. Kevin's machete was jammed in the side of his neck, severing his jugular. The homeless man stared at Jacob with hollow eyes, begging for help with his hopeless gaze—but to no avail.

Jacob tightly closed his eyes and lowered his head. He placed his hands over his ears, but he could still hear everything in the room. The nightmare wasn't over. The shuffling sound continued. The noise was followed by *clinking* and *crackling* sounds. The noise came from Jacob's belt and zipper. The sound of a *crinkling* wrapper emerged over the victim's groaning.

Jacob couldn't help himself. Again, he opened his eyes to a squint and stared at the cardboard bed. His vision was blurred, but he saw enough to recognize the violent attack. The bloodied machete sat on the floor beside the couple. A breeze swept an open condom wrapper across the floor.

The homeless man lay on his stomach, his legs spread wide. His pants were already removed, but his boots remained on his feet. He held his hands over the leaking gash on his throat as he stared at Jacob.

Kevin lay on top of the man as he thrust into his ass with all of his might. He kept one hand on the nape of the homeless man's neck, pushing him down to the ground. His other hand was firmly planted on the floor, helping him keep his balance. The violent teenager grunted and chuckled with each thrust, pleased by his actions.

Jacob closed his eyes and whimpered. Tears streamed down his cheeks, mucus dripped from his nostrils. The truth was irrefutable, he saw it with his own eyes, but he still couldn't believe it. His brother was raping a homeless man—that fact was jarring. *He can't be doing that,* he thought, *it's not possible.*

He felt numb. A tingling sensation covered every inch of his body, as if an army of ants were scurrying across his skin. He couldn't see or hear anything in the apartment. For a brief moment, he was whisked away from the cruel world. In a world of nothingness, he couldn't tell a second from a minute. He squirmed and gasped as he felt a tap on his shoulder—a gentle touch.

Jacob opened his eyes. His bottom lip quivered as he glanced around the room. The homeless man died with his eyes open. A puddle of blood formed under his head. Blood also stained his ass and thighs. A bloody, semen-filled condom sat on the floor beside the victim. The sight was horrific.

A crumpled bundle of newspaper burned in the corner, illuminating the living room. A crackling sound emerged from the fire. *When did he even start that? How long was I gone?*–Jacob thought.

Kevin grabbed Jacob's chin and turned his attention away from the victim. He said, "It's over. Don't look at him. Don't say a word."

Jacob gazed into Kevin's eyes, mystified. A contradicting mixture of guilt and pride lingered in his brother's eyes. He knew Kevin since the day he was born. In the abandoned building, surrounded by death and fire, he didn't recognize his own brother. He couldn't say a word. He thought: *who are you? What did you do with my real brother?*

Kevin said, "It's time to go home. Come on, walk ahead of me."

He grabbed Jacob's arm and helped him stand. He gently shoved him out of the apartment, trying to block his view of the murdered homeless man. Jacob followed his brother's instructions. He didn't kick or scream, he didn't complain or cry. Together, the siblings jogged out of the building and headed home.

Chapter Twelve

Another Morning

Jacob sat at the kitchen—quiet, exhausted, *traumatized.* He shoved a spoonful of cereal into his mouth as he scrolled through the local news on his cell phone. He had to find the aftermath of Kevin's crime to ease his anxiety. One of the headlines read: *Firefighters fight massive blaze at abandoned apartment building amid fears of homeless casualties.*

Kevin, on the other hand, sat quietly beside his younger brother. He ate his cereal while reading the back of the cereal box, unperturbed by his actions.

As she stirred her coffee near the stove, Isabel asked, "So, how was your weekend? You kids do anything fun?"

The siblings didn't respond. They weren't very talkative. They just continued slurping their cereal, oblivious of their mother's presence.

Isabel glanced over at the table with a furrowed brow, confused and worried. Silence was normal for Kevin, but Jacob usually enjoyed talking to her. She could only think of one reason for their silence: *they're angry about their punishment.*

She leaned back on the counter and asked, "Are you mad because I grounded you last week?" The boys remained quiet. Isabel sighed, then she said, "I'm sorry. I'm not sorry about grounding you because, well, you kinda deserved it. I *am* sorry for saying I was ashamed of you. I really didn't mean it. It was... It was just something stupid that slipped out. I had a bad day at work, I was tired of the calls from your schools, I... I just messed up. I'm sorry. Can you forgive me? *Please?"*

The brothers didn't say a single word. Isabel sighed in disappointment. She rubbed her temple with her fingertips as she felt the inevitable migraine creeping in. She took a sip of her coffee and tried to shrug it off. *They'll get over it,* she thought.

She asked, "Are you walking to school together again?"

Kevin chugged the milk in his bowl, then he said, "I can walk with him if he wants. It's not a problem for me."

As his family stared at him, Jacob lowered his head and gazed into the cold milk in his bowl. He couldn't stop thinking about the murders his brother committed. The violent rape and fire also clouded his mind. The grunting, groaning, squelching, and crackling sounds echoed through his head.

Jacob grunted to clear his throat, then he said, "I'll walk by myself today. I still have to get something from my room and... and I don't want you to be late, Kev."

Kevin shrugged and said, "Whatever." As he stood from his seat, he leaned closer to Jacob's ear and whispered, "We're in this together. Your hands are bloody, too. Remember that."

From the sink, Isabel said, "Bring your plates over. I'll wash 'em for you."

Jacob stood from his seat. He could see his brother smirking as he spoke to their mother, but he couldn't hear their words. The world around him was muted. He placed his bowl and spoon near the sink, then he withdrew to his bedroom.

In his room, he sat on his bed and riffled through his backpack. He didn't hear the sound of the front door slamming with Kevin's departure. He couldn't even hear the sound of rustling papers in his backpack.

Under his breath, he whispered, "What am I even doing?"

He thought about Dean's death. An image of bloody semen—thick and pink—jetting from a broken penis flashed in his mind. He sneered in disgust and shook his head. He was sickened by the violence, but he didn't feel horrible. He was burdened with conflicting emotions. He felt good for helping his brother slay a *real* monster. Dean was a convicted pedophile after all. Yet, he still felt bad for breaking the law and taking a life. He was an accomplice to a murder.

As he organized his worksheets, he whispered, "Did he deserve it? He did, didn't he? But... are we even allowed to do that? Is it okay to kill?"

Jacob took a deep breath and sniffled, fighting the urge to cry as he thought about the previous night. He thought about Kevin's barbaric actions. He raped and murdered an innocent homeless man. He couldn't justify his actions—it was impossible.

Kevin is evil, he thought, *he's the real monster.*

The idea broke his heart. He admired his older sibling. He pictured himself as a crime-fighter, fighting real villains with his brother. They were supposed to be real-life superheroes who slayed monsters like Dean. They weren't supposed to be serial killers.

He couldn't help but wonder if his brother was purposely manipulating him. He wanted to find a way to justify his brother's actions. He wanted to believe his brother was suffering from some split-personality disorder, like those he saw in horror movies. He didn't want to taint his brother's image.

Tears welling in his eyes, Jacob whispered, "What do you really want from me, Kev?"

From down the hall, Isabel yelled, "Jacob! Jacob, you almost ready for school, hun?"

Jacob wiped the tears from his eyes, then he closed his backpack. He stood up and tossed the bag over his shoulder. Before he could exit the room, Isabel stepped into his doorway.

She said, "Hey, sweetie, you're going to be late if you keep lollygagging. You might have to jog a few blocks.

Once again, Jacob didn't respond. For a moment —just a split-second—he thought about confessing to his mother. Yet, he couldn't throw Kevin under the bus, despite the booming voice of his conflicted conscience.

Isabel asked, "Are you okay, sweetie?" She placed her hand on his brow and said, "You don't feel hot. Does your head hurt? Is it your stomach?"

Jacob remained quiet. He loved his mother, he wanted to do the right thing, but he also wanted to stay out of trouble. He thought: *it doesn't matter anyway. If I tell on him, he'll tell on me, then we'll both end up in prison.*

Isabel caressed her son's cheek, then she asked, "Is this about your bully?"

Jacob glanced up at his mother with wide eyes. He asked, "You know about that?"

"Of course. What? Did you think I was just ignoring you? Did you think I couldn't see your bruises?"

"If you knew, why didn't you ever say anything?"

Isabel leaned on the doorway and frowned. She said, "It's complicated. I... I wanted *you* to take the first step. I didn't want to treat you like a baby 'cause I thought I would just make things worse for you. I figured you'd tell me when you couldn't keep things under control anymore."

"Oh..." Jacob responded, disappointed.

Isabel said, "I'm sorry if it feels like I haven't been doing enough for you. I think things will get better, though. Things always get better. Bullies never learn, but they get bored very quickly. So, you have a few options, hun. You can tell me about your bully and I can talk to that young man's parents for you or you can push through the punches and bad words. Whatever you want to do, I'm on your side."

Wyatt—Jacob didn't blurt out the name of his bully. He didn't agree with his mother, either. Her advice was outdated. Bullies evolved with the times. A bully could physically harm his victim at school, then continue the harassment online. And, thanks to the internet, a bully could follow his victim for years, regardless of location.

Wyatt had been bullying him since they were in kindergarten. The 'waiting game' wasn't working for him.

Isabel said, "Believe me, Jacob, things will get better for you in high school. There might still be some bullying here and there, but it won't be as bad. By the time you get to college, most of your classmates will forget about this childish nonsense and move on. Trust me."

You're lying—Jacob stopped himself before he could blurt out the response. College fraternities and sororities were often exposed for brutal hazing. He saw the videos online. In his mind, bullying and hazing were synonymous. Still, he found some comfort in his mother's optimistic words. He questioned her morals, but he still loved her. He felt like he wanted to protect her from bad people—people like Wyatt and Kevin.

Jacob said, "Thanks, mom. I should go to school now. I don't want to be late."

Isabel kissed his forehead, then she said, "Okay. Call me if you need anything. Love you."

"Love you, too."

Jacob walked out of the house, ready to start his day.

Chapter Thirteen

School is Hell

Monday, Tuesday, Wednesday, Thursday, Friday—the day didn't matter. School was always the same. The teachers were out of patience, most of the students didn't care about their classes, and everyone was just trying to finish the semester without losing their minds. Bullies roamed the halls with little consequence while victims lived in fear.

Same shit, different day.

As usual, Jacob sat at the back of the classroom. His English teacher was absent, so a lax substitute teacher took over the class. The substitute teacher only spoke to the students who were actually interested in the subject. The rest of the students were supposed to be reading and discussing a chapter from a literary novel. Instead, the students gossiped and argued while playing with their cell phones.

Jacob couldn't concentrate on the classwork. As a matter of fact, he didn't even bring his book to school so he couldn't participate. He quietly sat at his desk and doodled on an old worksheet—an assignment he never completed. He drew shadowy figures with machetes and baseball bats. He didn't have colored pencils, so he had to imagine the blood.

His mind was still dominated by the vicious

murders. He tried to forget about Dean and the homeless man, but he couldn't bury them. The men sat on his shoulders like angels and demons—except they were both demons. The deceased men tormented his conscience. His conscience said: *tell on your brother, free yourself from them.*

Jacob glanced over at the desk to his right. Molly Moore, his crush, sat beside him. The blonde-haired girl listened to music as she read the novel. Jacob considered telling her about his problems—*about his crimes.* He leaned closer and opened his mouth to speak, but he couldn't say a word. He stammered and groaned, but to no avail.

Upon spotting her classmate, Molly pulled an earbud out of her ear and asked, "You okay, Jacob?"

Jacob stuttered, "I–I... I don't know. I just... I–I wanted to–"

"Look, the faggot's having a seizure," Wyatt said from a seat to Jacob's left, causing the neighboring students to laugh. Mocking him, Wyatt stuttered, "You–You–You got a fucking speaking problem, Jacob? What? You need your slutty mom to talk for you?"

Jacob glared at Wyatt, fury burning in his eyes. He tightly clenched his number-two pencil as he thought about thrusting it into his neck. *Right through the jugular,* he thought, *I can make you bleed out like a pig.*

As he spotted Jacob's pencil, Wyatt chuckled, then he said, "Don't look at me like that, bitch. You're not going to do shit. You're a fuckin' pussy, just like your brother, and you're a bitch like your mom."

Before Jacob could respond, Molly said, "Leave him alone, Wyatt."

"Or what?" Wyatt asked.

"Or else."

Wyatt and his friends laughed, amused by the threat. The boys bickered and bantered. Some of the other bullies even teased Wyatt.

A boy said, "I didn't know you were scared of girls, Wyatt."

"*I'm not,*" Wyatt sternly said. He nodded at Molly and asked, "What can you do to me? Your mom is a crackhead, isn't she? She used to suck dick for crack when she was younger, right? Yeah, my dad told me about that. He knows all about the local whores."

Molly responded, "That's because your dad is always cheating on your mom. And, no, my mom doesn't do drugs. I think you're confusing her with your own mom."

"What did you say, bitch?"

Wyatt walked up to Molly's desk with his fists clenched. He towered over the petite girl as he wrestled with the urge to pummel her in front of the entire class. Brave and strong, Molly wasn't daunted by the threat of violence. She remained seated, glaring at the bully.

Molly asked, "What are you going to do? Are you going to beat me up in class in front of the sub? *Really?*"

Wyatt glanced over at the substitute teacher—he was still oblivious—then he glanced over at his classmates. The students at the back of the classroom kept their eyes on him. Some of the students even aimed their cellphones at the arguing pair, ready to record the fight for their favorite social media websites.

Wyatt huffed, then he said, "Whatever. I would beat the shit out of you if you weren't a girl. I'll get you back some other way, bitch. Don't worry about that." As he walked past Jacob, he whispered, "I'll get you back, too, punk. You're going to regret this."

Jacob was amazed by Wyatt's logic. The bully started the confrontation, but he acted as if he were wronged. He was a bully who was looking for vengeance against his victim.

As the students returned to their regular activities, Molly leaned closer to Jacob and asked, "So, what did you want to say?"

Jacob responded, "Never mind. It was nothing..."

"Are you sure?"

"Yeah. Thanks anyway. Thanks for everything."

Molly puckered her lips and nodded, then she said, "No problem. Let me know if you want to talk."

Jacob watched as Molly placed the earbud into her ear and continued reading. Again, he thought about telling her the truth. He couldn't muster the courage to confess, though. *If I can't say it, maybe I can write it,* he thought.

He pulled his cell phone out and scrolled through his contacts, searching for the perfect person. He chuckled inwardly as he stared at his phone, flicking his finger across the screen. His eyes welled with tears, his cheeks reddened. His contact list revealed his loneliness. He only had a handful of contacts—

his brother, his mother, and two classmates. He didn't speak to those classmates anymore, but he didn't delete their numbers. If he deleted their numbers, he felt as if he would be deleting his memories.

The harsh truth dawned onto him: he only had one true friend in life—*Kevin.* He couldn't text him, though. A killer's accomplice confessing to a killer would accomplish nothing. He didn't want to talk to him, either. He was afraid of enabling his brother's murderous behavior through their friendship.

The bell rang, disrupting his thoughts. The students scurried out of the classroom, ignoring the substitute teacher's reminder of the assignment.

As Jacob tossed his backpack over his shoulder, Molly said, "Jacob, wait." Jacob stopped and glanced back at his classmate. Molly approached him and said, "Hey, um... I was wondering if you wanted to hang out after school."

Awed, Jacob responded, "You want to hang out... with me?"

"Yeah. I know you had something to say and... and I want to say something to you, too. It's hard to talk with all of these people around, isn't it? So, can we hang out?"

Jacob rubbed the nape of his neck and said, "Well, I might be a little busy today."

"That's okay. I mean, I don't want to bug you or anything like that. But, um... I'll be home all day. So, if you want to drop by my house after school, that would be cool. It'll give us time to really talk. Besides, my parents won't be home until six or seven."

Jacob loudly swallowed the lump in his throat, then he stuttered, "I–I think I can be there..."

"Cool, cool. Do you, um... Do you want to eat lunch together?"

"I can't. I'm... I'm sorry. I already had some plans. Maybe tomorrow, okay?"

Molly smiled and said, "Okay. I'll see you later."

"Yeah, sure..."

Jacob and Molly exited the classroom, then they awkwardly split ways, ready to continue the rest of the tedious day.

***

Once again, Jacob sat by himself in the quad. He sat at his regular table and ate his regular microwavable burrito. He took a bite of his lunch and glanced around the area, searching for any signs of Molly. He lied to her about his plans so he didn't want her to see him. He was only surrounded by the same old cliques—cheerleaders, jocks, thugs, freaks, and geeks.

Anxiety swelling in his body, he whispered, "I have to get out of here."

He shoved his tray into the trash can, then he headed to the restroom. He walked with hurried steps, his shoulders raised and head down. He stayed away from the basketball courts in order to avoid his vicious bullies. Like a liberal in Hollywood, seamlessly blending with the crowds, he made it past his classmates without being noticed.

He sighed in relief as he entered the restroom. He glanced at the bottom of the stalls. To his dismay, the restroom was empty. Bad things always happened when the restroom was empty. He had nowhere else to go, so he went to the urinal and urinated. The sound of his piss hitting the urinal was unusually therapeutic. He felt at peace as he pissed. His shoulders relaxed, his arms loosened, and a smile formed on his face.

His anxiety was drained from his body with his piss. The sweet sensation of relief swept through his figure.

Jacob whispered, "It's okay. Everything's going to be okay."

As he walked towards the sinks to wash his hands, Wyatt appeared from behind the stalls and tackled Jacob. The bully rammed him with his shoulder, causing Jacob to clash with the wall at the end of the restroom.

Jacob turned and glared at his attacker, surprised and angry. Wyatt, Eric, and David stood before him. The restroom door was closed. An eerie feeling of déjà vu struck him. He thought about the piss on his hands, face, and shirt.

Jacob stepped forward and said, "Leave me alone, Wyatt. I don't want to–"

Mid-sentence, Wyatt struck Jacob with a quick jab. Jacob staggered back until he hit the wall again. He held his hand over his mouth and nose as he stared at Wyatt with wide eyes, awed. He expected a few insults and some urine, he didn't expect a punch. Violence was usually reserved for after-school bullying so they wouldn't get in trouble.

Jacob spotted the fury in Wyatt's eyes. He was

angry about the confrontation in their English class —and he was ready to exact his revenge.

Without saying another word, Wyatt punched Jacob again. Eric and David rushed forward and joined. The group of bullies pummeled him with a barrage of punches and kicks.

Jacob wrapped his arms around his head and fell to his knees. He couldn't withstand the force of their blows. He felt their knuckles and sneakers landing on his arms, ribs, and legs. A few of their strikes even slid past his arms and hit his head. Blood leaked from his nose and a small cut formed on his bottom lip.

Wyatt grabbed a fistful of Jacob's hair and said, "Get this bitch into the stall. Hurry up!"

Jacob cried as Wyatt pulled on his hair and dragged him across the restroom. He swung at Wyatt's arm, trying his best to break his grip, but to no avail. He was pushed into the first stall.

Wyatt kicked the toilet seat up, then he dunked Jacob's head into the water. Bubbling and gurgling sounds emerged as the water poured into his mouth and nose. Wyatt laughed as he pushed down on the lever, giving Jacob an old fashioned swirly. His fellow bullies patted his back and chuckled, as if they were congratulating him.

Jacob flailed his limbs as the water swirled around his head. His ears popped, his hair was pulled, and he struggled to breathe. He was dizzy and lightheaded. He felt as if he would faint at any moment. As the water returned, he lifted his head out of the bowl. He coughed, grunted, and spit as he struggled to catch his breath.

Wyatt beckoned to his friends and said, "David, hold him next to the toilet and cover his mouth. You too, Eric. Hurry up."

The stall walls rattled as the boys shifted positions. Jacob, exhausted and frightened, stood on his hands and knees in front of the toilet. His head hovered over the water and his chin rested on the rim of the bowl. David knelt down beside the toilet. He placed one hand over Jacob's mouth and the other on his shoulder, restricting his movements. Eric stood on the other side of the toilet. He placed his foot on Jacob's back and stopped him from moving.

Wyatt pulled a sharp number-two pencil out of his pocket and said, "I'm going to teach you a lesson you'll never forget, you fuckin' faggot."

Jacob's eyes widened as he felt his pants sliding down his legs. His boxers quickly followed. He felt a cool breeze on his ass. His heart pounded in his chest, his eyes were flooded with tears.

In a muffled tone due to David's hand, Jacob stuttered, "Pl–Please, don't... don't do this. I'm sorry. I'll never–"

Jacob gasped as Wyatt thrust the pencil into his ass. Veins bulged from his brow and neck, tears dripped from his bloodshot eyes. His arms and legs wobbled due to the insufferable pain. Wyatt pulled the pencil out an inch, then he thrust it deeper into his asshole. Only the eraser and the metal band protruded from his ass.

As Jacob wheezed and wept, Wyatt continued

thrusting the pencil in-and-out of his rectum. He sodomized him for thirty seconds. Blood leaked from his asshole and dribbled across his thigh.

Wyatt pulled the pencil out and staggered to his feet. With his fingertips, he held the pencil from its eraser. He held his other hand over his mouth as he examined the writing utensil. The other bullies grimaced in disgust, too. The pencil was painted red and brown with blood and feces. The sharpened lead also broke in Jacob's ass, trapped in his rectum.

Awed, Eric said, "Fucking gross, man..."

"Damn," David said as he stood up.

Without David's hand over his mouth, Jacob sobbed loudly. He wheezed and groaned, saliva dripping over his bottom lip. His tears and saliva dripped into the toilet water. His face was red from the pain, shock, and humiliation—as red as the blood leaking from his anus. He wanted to scream and fight, but he couldn't move.

Wyatt beckoned to his friends and said, "Move. Get out of the way." Again, the stall walls rattled as the boys moved in the tight space. Wyatt walked into the stall and said, "I told you I'd get you back, bitch."

The brawny bully kicked Jacob's face. Jacob fell to the floor beside the toilet, his jeans wrapped around his knees. He was dazed by the blow, barely conscious.

Wyatt sneered in disgust as he glared at his victim. He truly hated him. He threw the pencil away, then he approached the sinks. He casually washed his hands, unperturbed by his vicious crime. His friends joined him at the sinks. His friends, however, were rattled by the violence. They would never mess with Wyatt—they knew better.

As he watched Jacob from the reflection on the mirror, Wyatt said, "Jacob, you're not going to tell *anyone* about this. You hear me, punk? If you do, I'm going to fuck your mom. I'm going to make her bleed with my dick. And if she doesn't bleed, I'll just stick a knife up her pussy and watch her squirt some blood. So, keep your mouth shut and put your bitch on a leash. Punk..."

The bullies muttered and chuckled as they walked out of the restroom. Wyatt was proud of his actions. David and Eric were disgusted, but they still followed their leader.

Jacob whimpered and twitched as he lay on the cold floor, helpless and hopeless. He grabbed a piece of toilet paper and wiped the blood from his thigh. He didn't touch his stinging ass, though. He grimaced in pain as he lifted his pants up to his waist. He cried as he staggered to his feet. Every movement hurt him.

He walked with his legs wide apart, as if he were riding a horse. He stood in front of the sinks and stared at his reflection, ashamed. *Loser,* he thought, *you deserved it, you... you fucking faggot.* He couldn't help but hate himself. He sniffled as he washed his hands and face with lukewarm water. He couldn't wipe the bumps off of his head, he couldn't clean the bruises off of his face.

As he dried his hands and face with a paper towel, Jacob carefully examined his reflection on the mirror. He was bloodied and bruised, but his teachers wouldn't notice. He always had a few bruises. His wet hair was obvious, though. He looked as if he had just climbed out of the shower. He couldn't dry his hair with a paper towel after all.

He whispered, "I'm ready. I... I can do this."

He took a deep breath, then he walked out of the restroom. He stuck to the shadows, hiding from his classmates' prying eyes. No one looked his way, he was an insignificant person, but he still felt like all eyes were on him. He could hear his classmates snickering and gossiping about him. *I heard he was fucked with a pencil,* the voices said.

As he leaned on a wall behind a classroom, Jacob muttered, "Fuck all of you. You'll all pay for this. I swear, this isn't over."

He pulled his cell phone out. He stared at one name on his contact list: *Kevin.* After being brutalized in the restroom and abandoned by his classmates, he didn't have anyone else in the world. He sent his brother a text message that read: *He did it again. He fucked me up real bad.*

Within a minute, Kevin responded: *Wyatt??*

Jacob sniffled as he typed another message. The message read: *Yeah. He really fucked me up. I don't know what to do. Help me.*

Jacob covered his face with his hand as he sniveled. He tried to act strong around his classmates, but he was hurt and tormented. The attack scarred him—physically and mentally. He still felt the pain in his ass, too. The pain constantly reminded him of the attack. A minute felt like an hour as he waited for a response.

Jacob whispered, "Help me. Please, don't leave me like everyone else, Kev. Don't–"

His phone vibrated, interrupting his sad self-talk. He received another message from Kevin.

The message read: *Don't worry. I have a plan. I'll meet you after school.* (The message was followed by a smiling emoticon.)

Jacob sighed in relief. He didn't know what his brother was planning, but he trusted him. He was controlled by his lust for vengeance. The bell rang, calling Jacob to his next class.

Chapter Fourteen

How to Stop a Bully

"Did you see what Mrs. Richards was wearing today?" Wyatt asked as he walked home with his friends. He cupped his hands over his chest and enthusiastically said, "That shirt made her titties look *huge,* man! I couldn't stop staring at them."

Wyatt, David, and Eric walked home after school. The boys lived at the edge of town, a few blocks away from Jacob's house.

To the left, over the guardrail, there was a sea of trees—*the woodland.* The muddy ground was littered with autumn leaves, leaving the trees leafless. The guardrail protected the pedestrians and drivers from the short three-meter hill beside the sidewalk. To the right, there were streets upon streets of small, tumbledown houses.

Wyatt jogged in front of his friends and kicked an empty can on the sidewalk. He turned around and walked in reverse.

He said, "I think Richards saw me looking at them, too. You know, I think she's down to fuck."

David and Eric chuckled and shook their heads.

David said, "Come on, man. She's not that desperate."

"Besides, she's like forty years old," Eric added.

Wyatt shrugged and said, "I don't care. Forty or fourteen, it doesn't matter to me. I just wanna get laid already. My brother was getting pussy when he was thirteen, so I want to do it, too. Besides, man, Richards is hot as fuck. If you don't like her, you must be gay or something."

"Yeah, whatever," David muttered. He nodded at Wyatt and said, "We'll see you tomorrow."

Wyatt waved and turned around. He shouted, "Hit me up when you get home!"

The group split ways. Wyatt continued walking forward while David and Eric walked down a street to the right. A few teenagers walked up-and-down the sidewalk, their eyes glued to their phones. Every other minute, the sound of a coughing engine echoed through the street. It was a regular afternoon in the neighborhood.

"Wyatt!" a soft male voice shouted from the woods.

Wyatt stopped and furrowed his brow. He glanced over at the woodland, curious. He cracked a smile upon spotting Jacob at the bottom of the hill. Jacob stood with his hands behind his back, glaring up at the bully.

Wyatt leaned over the guardrail and asked, "How'd you get down there so quick? Did you really ditch school? Shit, I guess you're not such a–"

Jacob threw a brown paper bag up at Wyatt. Wyatt instinctively caught the bag with both hands. He jumped back and released the bag as soon as he felt its sopping wet texture. The bag also emitted a putrid stench—ammonia mixed with rotten eggs. *It's shit,* he thought, *he pissed on a bag full of shit and he actually threw it at me.*

He glared at Jacob and shouted, "Fuckin' punk!"

Without saying another word, Jacob sprinted into the woodland. He capered a bit, too, because of the pain emanating from his brutalized anus. Wyatt vaulted over the guardrail and slid down the hill.

As he ran into the woods, he shouted, "I'm going to kill you!"

Wyatt chased Jacob into a denser part of the woodland, running past tall trees and leafless shrubs. The boys ran nearly a quarter-mile away from the main road. Wyatt breathed noisily through his nose as he struggled to keep up. Jacob felt the ground vibrating under his feet. He felt as if a rhinoceros were chasing after him.

Jacob slid to a stop, then he turned around and walked in reverse until he bumped into a tree behind him. Wyatt stopped fifteen meters away from him, exhausted. Sweat dripping from his brow, the bully removed his jacket and took a moment to catch his breath.

Breathing heavily, Wyatt smiled and said, "I was going to leave you alone for a few days, Jacob. After that whole pencil thing, I was going to let you rest before I shoved my foot up your ass. I guess I'll do it now. I'm going to beat the shit out of you, bitch. I might even make you eat my shit after."

Smirking, Wyatt cracked his knuckles and marched towards Jacob. Jacob clenched his jaw and leaned back on the tree, ready to move forward with the plan.

Before Wyatt could reach Jacob, Kevin emerged from behind a tree, his head veiled by a ski mask. He swung an aluminum bat at Wyatt's right leg. The *clanging* sound of aluminum hitting bone echoed through the woodland, reverberating with Wyatt's bellow of pain.

Wyatt cried as he tumbled to the floor. He rolled onto his back and pulled his right knee up to his stomach. He hissed in pain as he rubbed his broken shin. His eyes widened with fear upon spotting his attacker. He recognized him even with the ski mask.

Tears streaming down his cheeks, he stuttered, "Wha–What the fuck, man? What... What are you doing?" He glanced down at Kevin's bat and sobbed. He cried, "Don't hurt me. Pl–Please, we... we were just messing around. Tell him, Jacob. Tell... Tell him it was all a game. Please–"

Kevin struck down at Wyatt's right kneecap. The bat *clanged* and vibrated with the blow. Wyatt moved his hands up to his busted kneecap. Unfortunately, Kevin wasn't finished with him. He struck down and hit Wyatt's hand, breaking his bones upon impact.

Wyatt squirmed in reverse and cried, "Please stop! *I'm sorry!*"

Kevin shouted, "Shut the fuck up!"

The murderous teenager moved closer to the bully, then he struck down at Wyatt's right thigh. He didn't break any bones, but he definitely bruised his leg. He lifted the bat over his head, then he swung down at his ankle. Wyatt howled and convulsed on the floor as the bat fractured his ankle.

As planned, Kevin mangled Wyatt's right leg with the brutal swings. Wyatt lay on his back on the muddy ground, his t-shirt and jeans stained with mud. He placed his good hand on his injured knee and lifted his broken hand up to Kevin, as if to say: *please stop, it hurts.*

Grunting and groaning, Wyatt weakly said, "Please, don't do this. I... I said I was sorry. It was... It was stupid, okay? I–I know that now, man, I get it. I won't bother him again, I swear." He started to hyperventilate, panting like a pregnant woman in labor. He grimaced and cried, "Call 911. Tell 'em I'm out here. I won't tell on you. You have my word. O–Okay? We–We're good. Just don't hurt me anymore. Please, man, *please.*"

Kevin bent over and said, "*No.* For years, I watched my brother come home with cuts and bruises. *For years,* I listened to my little brother cry himself to sleep at night because of all of the shit you put him through. I'm tired of seeing people like my brother getting hurt by people like you. I'm sick and tired of seeing you act like you're the top dog of this place. Well, I've got news for you, punk: *you're not.* I'm at the top of the food chain—and I'm going to put you in your place."

"Wha–What?"

"I'm going to make an example out of you. You have to be punished."

Kevin held the bat over his head, then he swung down at Wyatt. He repeatedly struck his hip, his arm, and his leg. Wyatt yelped with each blow. He flailed his limbs every which way as he tried to squirm away, but to no avail.

From the tree, Jacob watched the brutal beating

in utter awe. He had already witnessed his brother's viciousness through the murders of Dean and the homeless man. It was different with Wyatt, though. Although he was violent and obnoxious, Wyatt was a kid just like him—young and foolish. He couldn't listen to his cries.

Jacob lurched forward and yelled, "Stop! That's enough! We got him, okay? It's over! Please, stop!"

To his dismay, Kevin couldn't stop himself. He swung down and struck Wyatt's stomach with the bat, knocking the air out of him. He held the bat over his head, grinning as he aimed at Wyatt's dome. *Smash his skull,* he thought, *make his brains ooze out.* The idea made him feel giddy like a child meeting a mall Santa Claus for the first time.

Before he could hit him, Jacob ran forward and pushed Kevin. He jumped and pulled the ski mask off of his brother's head, revealing his face.

Jacob shouted, "*There!* He knows who you are. He can tell the cops, he can tell a judge, he can... he can tell everyone. You can't do this, Kev! He knows who you are! *You* know who you are! This isn't you, man. Please, don't do this..."

"He recognized me the moment I first hit him. I just told him you were my little brother. He always knew it was me, idiot," Kevin responded, smirking. He huffed and shook his head, amused by his little brother's attempt to stop him. He said, "But, you're right. He knows who we are, little man. That gives us a reason to kill him. He's seen me, he's seen you. Really, *you* should be dealing with him. Kill him, Jacob. Show him who's the real boss around here.

Make him your bitch. Put him in his place."

Teary-eyed, Jacob said, "This isn't what I wanted. I don't want to kill him. I never wanted to do this! I just... I wanted to teach him a lesson, but not like this. I just wanted to scare him. That's all."

Kevin sighed and looked up at the trees, frustrated. The tree branches waved at him with each gust of wind. While they argued, Wyatt started crawling away from the siblings. The leaves rustled under his weight and he grunted with the slightest movement, but he was able to crawl without being noticed. He dragged his broken leg behind him.

Kevin glanced back at his brother and responded, "Scare him? *Scare him?* Are you kidding me? Scaring him won't stop him from fucking you with a knife."

"It was a pencil," Jacob said, his head down in shame.

"It doesn't matter. If you want the bullying to stop, you have to *make* it stop. You have to teach him, and everyone like him, a lesson. You have to kill him."

"I can't."

"You have to, Jacob."

"I can't!"

"You can!"

The sound of a *snapping* twig emerged in the woods. The arguing siblings glanced over their shoulders. Wyatt accidentally crawled over a twig a few meters away from the brothers.

As he approached the bully, Kevin muttered, "This fat piece of shit. Who the hell does he think is?" He kicked Wyatt's shoulder, forcing the bully to roll onto his back. He asked, "Where's your pencil? Hmm? Where is it? I have to show you something."

Wyatt wiggled on the ground like a worm in mud. Mouth overflowing with saliva, he cried, "Please, stop... It hurts, man. I–I need to go to a hospital."

As Kevin tapped Wyatt's pants, patting him down like a cop during a drug search, Jacob approached and said, "I'm not going to stay here with you, Kev. I'm supposed to meet Molly today. I... I have to go. I'm sorry."

"Here it is," Kevin said as he pulled a clean number-two pencil out of Wyatt's pocket. "You fucked my brother with a pencil. I'm not going to do the same 'cause that won't kill you. You deserve worse anyway."

Wyatt shook his head and yelled, "No! Please!" He glanced over at Jacob and shouted, "Fuck, I'm sorry! Please, man, don't let him do this! Stop him! Help me! Somebody, *help.* He's–"

He stopped as Kevin knelt down beside him. The murderous teenager held the pencil over his head with the tip pointing downward. He stared at the sharp tip of the pencil, eyes wide with fear. At that moment, his life flashed before his very eyes. He screamed at the top of his lungs.

Jacob rushed forward and pushed his brother, causing Kevin to tumble to the floor. Kevin glared at Jacob, irritated by his interruptions.

Jacob said, "Don't do this, Kev. I'm begging you."

From the ground, Kevin kicked Jacob's stomach. Jacob held his hands over his stomach as he teetered left-and-right. Kevin jumped to his feet, then he struck his brother with a swift jab. Jacob lost his balance and fell to the ground. Kevin hit him with a barrage of punches—left, right, left, right. His little brother was dazed by the attack.

Kevin said, "Wait here and watch this."

Jacob mumbled, "I–I... I can't... You can't do this, Kev. It... It's wrong."

"It's the right thing to do. Remember, I'm doing this for your own good. Don't worry, you can still see your little girlfriend later. I just want you to watch this first."

Jacob grunted as he crawled in reverse. He leaned back on a tree behind him as he watched his brother approach his bully. *What are you going to do?*–he thought.

As he knelt down beside Wyatt, Kevin said, "I should have done this to your brother, too."

"Wait, man. Please, let me–"

Kevin thrust the pencil into Wyatt's right eye. Bodily fluids—blood, tears, and a thick gel-like substance—spurted from his eye and poured over his eyelid. His vision quickly faded as his eye hemorrhaged. Wyatt shrieked and convulsed, shocked by the jolting pain. He swung at Kevin's arms, but to no avail.

Kevin turned his wrist and, in turn, he twisted the pencil in his eye socket—as if he were manually sharpening a pencil. More fluids dripped from his eye. Then, the pencil *snapped* in half. One half of the pencil protruded from Wyatt's eye, like a legendary sword trapped in a stone. It was good for Kevin, though. It meant he didn't have to find another weapon to hurt Wyatt.

Kevin thrust the other half of the pencil into Wyatt's left eye. The splintered wood easily penetrated his eye, too. Bloody tears streamed down his rosy cheeks.

Wyatt breathed throatily as he rolled in pain. He couldn't see, he couldn't scream, and he couldn't stand up. He was essentially blinded and paralyzed by the attack. Hoarse breaths escaped his lips as he struggled to breathe. His leg violently trembled and saliva foamed in his mouth. He went into shock and choked on his tongue.

Kevin grinned and said, "You fat fuck, you're going to die trying to swallow more than you can chew... Shit, that looks painful. I wouldn't want to go out like that."

Wyatt stopped shaking. His chest didn't rise, his stomach didn't move. He stopped breathing. Aside from an involuntary twitch here and there, the young teenager stopped moving entirely. He passed away due to the shock.

Kevin glanced over at Jacob and said, "It's over. He won't bother you anymore."

Jacob remained quiet—sad, scared, *shocked*. He watched as his brother covered Wyatt's body with the autumn leaves. Kevin pulled a water bottle out of his backpack, then he rinsed the blood off of his gloves. He washed the baseball bat, too.

Kevin approached his brother and said, "Come on, it's time to go." Awed, Jacob continued to stare at Wyatt's body, which was hidden in plain sight. Kevin grabbed Jacob's arm and pulled him to his feet, then he said, "It's okay. Everything is fine. I'm sorry for hitting you. I just lost my cool. It won't happen again. Alright? You okay?"

Jacob blankly stared forward and whispered, "I have to see Molly. She... She wants me to go to her house. She wants to talk to me. I have to see her..."

"Yeah, you're going to see her. And you're going to be confident, too. You know why?"

Jacob remained motionless and quiet.

Kevin continued, "It's because this nightmare is over. You don't have to worry about Wyatt and his shit anymore. You can finally feel safe."

Tears dripping from his eyes with each blink, Jacob nodded and repeated, "I have to see her."

Kevin sighed in disappointment. He never planned on harming his little brother, mentally or physically. Through his sorrowful eyes, he could see the scars on his soul. He gently shook his brother and smiled, trying to keep a semblance of control.

He said, "Let's get out of here before someone sees us. Come on."

Kevin grabbed his brother's arm and jogged away from the crime scene, leading his brother away from the desolate woodland.

Chapter Fifteen

What If I Were A Bad Person?

Silence—Jacob and Kevin walked home without saying another word. They strolled past their neighbors and occasionally waved 'hello' to their acquaintances. A boy was beaten to death in the woods, but the world still moved at the same pace. A mother anxiously waited for her child to return home, her mind flooded with horrific possibilities, but that didn't matter to anyone else.

Tragedy was not universal, sadness was not shared—*unless* it was popular on social media.

Jacob sniffled as he walked through a gate to his left. He was nervous about his 'date' with Molly, but he would do anything to get away from his homicidal brother. Kevin grabbed Jacob's backpack and pulled him back to the gate. He seemed serious and concerned, stony-faced. The brothers glared at each other for a moment.

In a soft tone, just above a whisper, Kevin said, "I know you're angry at me. That's fine. We can deal with that later. I just want you to know one thing: we *both* go down if you snitch. Talk to her about anything you want—movies, music, video games, fuckin' unicorns—but *don't* talk to her about what we did and what we do. Okay?"

Jacob stared at his brother. *You're not the same,* he thought, *or maybe I'm just seeing you for the first time.* He could only appease his brother by nodding in agreement.

Kevin said, "Good. I'll be waiting for you at home. Call me if you need anything."

"S–Sure..."

The brothers split ways. Jacob strolled up the walkway and approached the front door of the house, Kevin walked to the end of the cul-de-sac and headed home.

Jacob knocked on the door. He stared down at himself as he waited. Due to the scuffle with his brother in the woods, dirt stained his windbreaker and his jeans. There was a small bump over his right eye and a cut on his lip, too.

The door swung open. Molly stood in the doorway, happy and excited. The smile on her face slowly turned into a frown as she examined Jacob's injuries. He looked normal during their English class.

Nervous, Molly said, "Hey, Jacob. Are you okay?"

Jacob smiled and said, "I'm okay. I just... Don't worry about it. You, um... you wanted to talk, right?"

"Yeah. You came a little later than I thought, so my parents might be home soon."

Jacob lowered his head and said, "I'm sorry..."

"No, it's okay. We can still talk for a few minutes," Molly responded. She grabbed Jacob's hand and pulled him into her house. As she locked the door behind him, she said, "Come on, we can sit down in my room. If my parents come home, you can just climb out the window."

Jacob glanced around the living room, curious.

The house reminded him of his own home. He couldn't help but smile as he spotted the photographs in the picture frames. The pictures depicted a happy family. For some reason, he wasn't jealous of them. Their happiness was contagious. *Maybe I'm not bad,* he thought, *maybe I just need better friends.*

Molly held Jacob's hand and led him down a hallway. They entered the second room to the right —Molly's room.

Molly said, "Come on. Let's sit on my bed."

Jacob looked away from Molly and grimaced as he sat on the bed at the other end of the bedroom. He didn't want her to ask about the pain in his ass, so he couldn't let her see his expression of agony.

As Molly sat down beside him, he looked around the room. Posters of pop stars clung to the light blue walls. Balls of dust rolled across the hardwood floor. Photo booth pictures of friends and family sat on her dresser. Her computer was open to a page about history for a school assignment. It was a normal room for a teenage girl.

Jacob and Molly glanced at each other. They smiled, giggled, and blushed. The silence was awkward but expected.

Molly said, "So... did you finish the English homework? I didn't see you reading in class so I thought you probably already finished it."

Jacob stared down at his lap and said, "Nope. I just forgot my book at home."

"Oh... Well, if you ever want to work on it together, just let me know. It's pretty boring doing homework alone, right?"

"Yeah, I guess so."

"It'll be easier, too. You can read a chapter, I'll read a chapter, then we'll just go over the questions together."

"Yeah, that... that sounds good."

Once again, the couple sat in an awkward silence. Molly stared at her classmate with a set of worried eyes. Jacob twiddled his thumbs and avoided eye contact.

Molly asked, "What did you want to say to me in class?"

I wanted to talk about murder—the truth was violent, disturbing, and illegal. He couldn't confess, so he bit his tongue and kept it to himself.

"Nothing," Jacob responded.

"When you talked to me in class, I thought it was serious. It was just a... I don't know, I just saw a look in your eyes. You looked hurt, you know? Was it about Wyatt?"

Jacob glanced over at Molly, wide-eyed. An image of Wyatt's dead body flashed in his mind. His vision reddened, as if blood were cascading over his eyelids. He tightly closed his eyes, then he opened them. To his utter relief, his vision returned to normal.

He stuttered, "Wy–Wyatt?"

"Everyone knows that he bullies you. It's obvious. I even heard a teacher talking about it once. He just didn't do anything to help. 'It's just boy stuff, it's part of life,' he said. I don't think it's normal, though. It's not right. Look at your bruises and cuts... We're supposed to be safe in school, aren't we?"

Molly continued to babble about the injustices that occurred in school. Jacob didn't hear her words, though. He was more concerned with his own complicity in the deaths in the neighborhood. He thought: *are the cops looking for Dean's killer? Do they know about the homeless man? Have they already found Wyatt? Do they know about me?*

Interrupting Molly, Jacob asked, "Can I ask you a question?"

Molly nodded and said, "Sure. What is it?"

"What do you think of the world?"

Molly forced a smile and nervously asked, "*What?*"

"Do you believe in... in good and evil?"

"I guess. I mean, some people do good things so they're good and some people do bad things so they're bad—or evil. Right?"

Jacob gazed into Molly's eyes and said, "That's what I thought, too. I was just wondering because... Well, someone told me that we were brainwashed to believe that sort of stuff—to believe in good and evil. He told me that... that we should be free to kill if we wanted to because everyone wants to kill someone. Do you think that's true?"

Molly stared at Jacob with a deadpan expression. She covered her mouth and burst into a giggle, rocking back-and-forth on the bed.

She said, "I think you should stop listening to whoever told you that 'cause it's not true. Only psychos want to kill innocent people, Jacob, so you might be talking to some crazy kid or something.

You should tell his parents or a teacher or *someone.* It's just... It's crazy."

The couple laughed together. Jacob nervously smiled and nodded, as if to say: *yeah, you're right, I was just kidding.* The laughter dwindled to some snickering, then the room became quiet. Their eyes darted left-and-right as they awkwardly waited for the next word.

Jacob hopped and gasped as Molly grabbed his hand. He stared at her hand, then up at her face, then back at her hand. He never held hands with a girl before.

As the couple locked eyes, Molly said, "I like you, Jacob. I mean, I like-*like* you."

Jacob cocked his head back, amazed. He liked her since the fifth grade. After living through such a cruel and unfair life, he never thought he'd have a chance at dating Molly—he never thought he'd have a chance at true happiness. Tears welled in his eyes, butterflies fluttered in his stomach. He wanted to pinch himself to make sure he wasn't dreaming, but he knew that would be silly.

He coughed to clear his throat, then he asked, "Would you still like me if I were bad?"

"What do you mean?"

"You know, good and evil... What if I wasn't good? What if I were a bad person?"

"I guess I wouldn't like you... But, you're *not* a bad person, Jacob. I can see it in your eyes. You might have bad thoughts because of the bad things kids do to you, but you're not bad. You're, um... You're one of the good ones. You're nice, you're sweet... *you're good."*

Jacob was baffled by Molly's explanation. His brother saw something different in his eyes. Kevin's words echoed through his mind: *I see anger in your eyes, I see hatred in your soul.* It didn't make sense to him. *How could they see different things in my eyes?*– he thought. Once again, he questioned his brother's intentions and his own murderous thoughts.

Jacob stared down at himself and said, "I was wrong. I was totally wrong. I'm not like him. I... I made a mistake."

"What are you talking about?" Molly asked. "A mistake? Don't you like me, too?"

Jacob shook his head as he snapped out of his contemplation. He nodded and said, "I like you. I really like you, Molly. I just... I did something bad with my brother. He... He tricked me, you know? I have to stop him from doing anything else."

"Okay, um... I think I understand. Do you need my help?"

"I don't know. I just... I need to think."

Jacob considered telling her about everything— about Dean, about the homeless man, about Wyatt. He figured she could tell her parents about Kevin and her parents could tell the police. He couldn't risk it, though. He was an accomplice and Kevin wouldn't let him forget that. Family issues had to be handled by family.

Jacob said, "No, I don't think I need your help. I have to do this by myself. I have to fix my own problems for once."

Molly nodded—*okay.* She leaned forward and

kissed Jacob's cheek. Jacob's eyes widened as he felt her soft lips on his face. It wasn't a kiss on the lips, but he figured it counted as his first kiss. The couple shared a smile.

Jacob stood up and said, "I should go. I'll talk to you at school. If... If I don't show up, I just want you to know: it was all a... a mistake. I just messed up. Thanks for everything. And, um... and I *really* like you, Molly."

Molly blushed and said, "I like you, too." As Jacob took a step forward, Molly said, "And, Jacob, as long as you try to fix your problem, I think you'll be okay. Your heart is good. I mean, whatever you did... it can't be *that* bad anyway, right?"

Jacob glanced back at Molly. *It's very bad*—the words were trapped in his throat. He forced a smile and nodded, then he left her house and rushed home.

Chapter Sixteen

A Family Dinner

Jacob stood in the bathroom, vigorously washing his hands with boiling water in the sink. He rubbed a bar of soap on his fingernails and palms, then he held his hands under the water. He repeated the process over and over—and over again. Like a person with an obsessive-compulsive disorder, he couldn't stop washing his hands.

He whimpered and sniffled as the scalding water burned his hands. His skin reddened and wrinkled. He rubbed the bar of soap on his hands, hoping it would soothe his pain, but it didn't work. He figured he deserved it anyway. Through his teary eyes, he saw blood on his hands—the blood of his brother's victims. So, he continued rubbing his hands under the hot water.

You're one of the good ones—Molly's words echoed through his mind. He stopped washing his hands and stepped in reverse. Tears welling over in his eyes, he stared at his reflection on the mirror.

He whispered, "I'm one of the good ones. I *am* one of the good ones. Kevin, he lied to me. That... that asshole. I should have never trusted him."

He glanced over his shoulder upon hearing the sound of the front door slamming. He turned the faucet off, then he wiped his hands with a towel. His sensitive fingers, red and swollen, stung with the slightest touch.

"Jacob! Kevin!" Isabel called out from the front door. "Come on! The food is here!"

"Food?" Jacob repeated in disbelief. As he walked out of the bathroom, he whispered, "When was the last time she bought take-out?"

Jacob walked down the hall with his head down, nervous and afraid. He stopped near the kitchen archway and stood beside his brother. The siblings stared at the front door, surprised. Their differences were temporarily set aside due to the revelation.

Isabel stood near the front door, a box of pizza in her hands. The woman wore a tight dress, which revealed her large breasts and succulent legs. Her high heels propelled her to a five-six stature. Clearly, she did *not* spend her day at work. The brothers weren't exactly surprised by her outfit, though. They were caught off guard by the man standing beside their mother.

The middle-aged man was charismatic and handsome. He wore a white button-up shirt with the sleeves rolled up to his elbows, gray slacks, and dress shoes. His slick black hair was combed over to the side, waxed to perfection. He appeared to be lean and strong.

Jacob recognized the glimmer in his eyes, though —a glimmer of deviance. His zany eyes resembled Kevin's eyes. From his aura, he could tell he wasn't a nice person. He only wanted sex—rough, nasty sex. His mere presence was also surprising. Isabel constantly brought men home, but she usually waited until after dark to sneak them into the house. Her actions were highly unusual.

Upon noticing the new bruises and bumps on Jacob's face, Isabel asked, "Jacob, are you okay? What happened to you, baby? Was it–"

"He's okay. We already talked about everything and I'm going to help him. Don't worry about it," Kevin interrupted. Unusually stern, he nodded at the man and asked, "Who's this guy?"

Isabel smiled as she glanced over at her guest. In an instant, her concerns about her bullied son were swept away.

She said, "Boys, this is Luke—Luke Keller. You can call him Mr. Keller, but I'm sure he wouldn't mind if you called him Luke." She glanced over at the man and asked, "Is that okay?"

Luke smiled and said, "Of course. I don't mind at all. It's nice to finally meet the kids."

The brothers remained quiet as they stared at the couple.

Isabel nervously laughed, then she said, "He's, um... He's my boyfriend. We're a couple. You understand?"

Jacob bit his bottom lip and nodded. He didn't care about his mother's search for love, but Luke brought an element of uncertainty to the equation. He didn't know how to confront his brother with the man in their house.

Kevin lowered his head. Under his breath, he muttered, "Looks different from the guy last night..."

"You say something, baby?" Isabel asked. Kevin shook his head. Isabel said, "*Anyway,* I can see you boys are shy. So, I'll introduce you. The older one is

Kevin and the younger one, my baby boy, is Jacob."

Luke grinned and said, "Kevin and Jacob... That's easy enough to remember."

"Yeah. Don't worry, they'll come around," Isabel responded. She beckoned to her children and said, "Let's get this pizza to the kitchen and start eating before it gets cold. Jacob, baby, please set the table for four. Luke is joining us tonight."

Jacob nodded in agreement, then he shambled into the kitchen. Kevin smirked at his mother as he grabbed the box of pizza. Isabel and Luke stood near the front door and chatted about the awkward first impression.

***

Jacob set the table with four plates and four cups. He placed a two-liter bottle of soda and a roll of paper towels on the table. *Voila!*—the table was set.

Jacob and Kevin sat on one side of the table while Isabel and Luke sat on the other. They didn't say grace. They didn't even share another word. Through the awkward silence, they each grabbed a slice of pizza.

As he chewed on his food, Luke held his hand over his mouth and said, "I hear you're still in school—high school and middle school. It's been a while since I've been in a classroom. How is it? You have any favorite subjects? Or do you just hate them all?"

The brothers didn't respond. Kevin glared at the man as he ate, blatantly angry. Jacob picked at his food, pulling the mushrooms off of the hot cheese. Luke took another bite of his slice and shrugged.

Isabel said, "This is... awkward, isn't it? I mean, I get it: it's always weird meeting your mom's boyfriend. You just need to let it happen, though. You need to give us a chance. We can't succeed if you don't give us a chance."

Luke dabbed the sides of his mouth and said, "Maybe you should tell 'em how we met."

"Yeah, sure. That sounds like a good idea. You boys wanna know how we met?"

Again, the siblings remained quiet.

Isabel blushed and scooted forward in her seat. She said, "Well, it's a funny story. A few weeks ago, my car broke down before I could get to work. I don't have AAA, I couldn't get anyone on the phone, so I tried to wave people down. You should have seen me. I looked like a crazy woman out there. I don't blame people for driving past me... *One* person stopped, though." She pointed at Luke and smiled. She continued, "Luke stopped by and helped me. Well, he *tried* to help. It turns out: he couldn't fix the problem, either. But, he picked me up, he gave me a ride to work, and he promised me the car would be working once I got out. And, he kept his promise. Ever since then, we've been talking on the phone, going out on small dates... We've been a couple."

Jacob watched his mother with narrowed eyes. He could see the love in her eyes as she gazed at her new boyfriend. Yet, he still couldn't properly read Luke's personality. *I can't judge him so fast,* he thought, *maybe everyone isn't as bad as Kevin says.*

"How is that a 'funny' story?" Kevin asked, staring at his mother with a deadpan expression.

Isabel stuttered, "Wha–What?"

"You said it was a funny story. It sounds like your car broke down, this guy picked you up, and you started dating. What's so funny about that? Where's the punchline?"

"Well, um... I meant 'funny' as in, like... It's just funny how things work out, you know?"

"No, I don't. I really don't."

Kevin shoved the rest of his pizza into his mouth, devouring his food. He tossed another slice onto his plate, ready to continue his feast.

As he chewed, he said, "Anyway, it may not be *funny*, but it was a nice story, mom. I mean, it's better than the rest of 'em. Guys usually pick you up like a cheap hooker on the back pages, right?"

Isabel held her hands over her mouth and gasped. She was shocked and offended by the crass comment. Her son—her own flesh and blood— verbally attacked her.

Luke said, "Whoa, whoa, whoa. That's your mother, kid. Show her some respect."

Kevin huffed, then he said, "Don't talk to me like that, man. You're not my dad. Why the hell should I listen to you?" He chuckled and shook his head, amused. He said, "Actually, you *could* be my dad. Shit, man, anyone in this city could be my dad. What is that old saying? Finding him is like... like finding a needle in a haystack. Listen, *Luke,* my mom has fucked *every* man in the city, except for me and my brother. I don't know if we're lucky or unlucky for that."

Isabel opened her mouth to speak, but she

couldn't utter a word. An insult from a close family member felt like a stab in the back. Jacob watched the confrontation with a furrowed brow. He couldn't understand his brother's intentions. *What are you planning? Are you actually angry?*–he thought.

Luke wagged his finger at Kevin and sternly said, "Alright, that's enough. I'm not going to sit here while you insult your mother like this."

"Then leave!" Kevin shouted.

"I'm not leaving, either. I'm here to stay. You understand me, boy?"

"Boy? *Boy?* I'm almost eighteen, you dumb fuck."

Luke slammed his fist on the table and barked, "Go to your room!"

"What?! This is *my* house! You don't get to make the rules around here!"

"If you can't act like a civilized person, if you can't respect your mother, you should leave. Go to your room and cool down, kid."

Kevin sneered in annoyance and said, "Fuck you and fuck her."

Kevin threw his slice of pizza at Luke. The pizza hit Luke's face, then it fell onto his shirt. Luke stood up and glared at the psychopathic teenager. Kevin wasn't daunted by the challenge, either. He stood up, ready to fight with the man.

As Luke took his first step around the table, Kevin glanced over at the kitchen counter. Jacob could see Kevin was looking at the knife block. He thought: *he's actually going to stab him to death for no reason, he's the real monster.*

Jacob lunged forward and grabbed Kevin's arm.

He pulled his brother away from the counter, stopping him before he could even reach for a knife.

Before Luke could reach them, Isabel stood from her seat and shouted, "Enough!" The boys stopped moving and stared at her. Isabel said, "You're right, Kevin. Luke doesn't make the rules in this house. He has no right to act like your father. You just met him. I can't expect you to treat him like a dad."

Luke rubbed the nape of his neck and sighed in disappointment. Caught in the moment, he didn't realize he was only aggravating the situation with his interference. Kevin smiled smugly. The type of smile that said: *I told you so.*

Isabel said, "*But,* you're also wrong, Kevin. You don't make the rules, either. It's *my* house, you're *my* kids, so I make the rules. I want you both to go to your rooms. *Now.*"

As he walked away, Kevin whispered, "Whatever."

Jacob glanced over at his mother, then at Luke. He didn't say another word. He walked back to his room. He could hear Luke apologizing to his mom. He didn't think much of it. He locked the door, then he fell onto his bed and cried into his pillow. Thoughts of Kevin dominated his mind. He recalled his brother's vile rants verbatim, he remembered every detail of their violent murders, and he thought about his role in the world.

Good and evil, love and hatred, life and death, family and enemies—ideas flooded his mind, but he couldn't think clearly. It was like listening to a hundred overlapping voices and trying to identify a single person. As he tried to cry himself to sleep, one question echoed through his mind: *what the hell am I going to do now?*

Chapter Seventeen

A Night of Mayhem

Incest was immoral and deviant. Throughout most of the United States, incest was downright illegal, even between consenting adults. Yet, faux-incest porn was incredibly popular to certain perverted people—and Kevin was one of those perverts. However, the deviant teenager didn't have to settle for poorly-acted or foreign porn videos to get his fix.

Kevin stood in his closet, his boxers wrapped around his ankles and his hand glued to his dick. His body was drenched in sweat from head-to-toe. He panted and groaned. The closet was cramped and claustrophobic, he could hardly breathe in the hot storage room, but he liked it. The lack of oxygen aroused him.

Through the peephole, he peeked into his mother's bedroom. He watched his mother fuck her new boyfriend. Isabel stood on all fours, facing the foot of the bed, while Luke thrust into her from behind—*doggystyle.* His mother loudly moaned and wildly shook her head, pleased by the sex. Her breasts jiggled with each thrust and he could see her ass since her back was arched down.

What a view.

"Just like that," Isabel said, her voice cracking with pleasure. "Don't stop. Please, don't stop. I'm almost–"

Isabel paused and stared at her closet with a furrowed brow. She still moaned with pleasure, but she couldn't concentrate. She heard something else in the room. Her eyes locked on the closet, she pulled away from Luke and stood on her knees on the bed.

She tapped Luke's chiseled abs and said, "Wait."

Luke asked, "What? What's wrong? Did I hurt you? Was I–"

Isabel held her index finger up to Luke's lips—*shush.* She placed her finger under her earlobe, communicating with her gestures: *do you hear that?* Luke tilted his head and raised his brow, confused. After ten seconds of silence, he narrowed his eyes and nodded. A faint *squelching* sound seeped into the bedroom.

Luke whispered, "What is that? An animal?"

"I think it's coming from the closet," Isabel responded.

She staggered off of the bed and slipped into her robe, then she turned on the lamp on the nightstand. As she tied her robe, she walked towards the closet. Meanwhile, Luke muttered to himself and slipped into his boxer briefs.

The *squelching* sound grew louder with each passing second.

Isabel leaned into the closet. Her eyes widened with shock. She could finally see the hole at the back of her closet. The pieces were easy to connect: the noise was coming from the hole and the hole led to Kevin's closet. She only knew one action that could create such a noise, too.

Still, she needed irrefutable proof to believe such a disgusting revelation. She leaned closer to the hole, trying to peek into the neighboring closet.

She stuttered, "Ke–Kevin, is... is that you, baby? You–You're not in your closet, are you?"

The racket continued, but Kevin didn't respond. Before she could utter another word, Kevin loudly grunted and the wall trembled. Streams of cum jetted through the peephole. The gooey semen hit the bottom of his mother's coats and dripped down to the floor.

Isabel gasped and stepped in reverse—shocked, disgusted, *infuriated.* She could tell semen from glue, so she knew what her son did in the closet.

She stomped and shouted, "Kevin White! That better be fake!"

As he stared at the cum, Luke sneered in disgust and whispered, "What the fuck?"

"Thanks for the nut, mom," Kevin said as he lifted his underwear up to his waist, smirking.

Kevin chuckled as he casually walked out of the closet. Time was not of the essence. As a matter of fact, he wanted to prolong the event for as long as possible. He wanted to remember every detail of the night, he wanted to cherish the memories for the rest of his life.

Wearing only his boxers, Kevin walked into the hallway. At the same time, his mother barged out of her bedroom and shambled into the hall. She tightened the robe, trying her best to cover her body. She was completely nude under the robe after all.

Scowling, Isabel approached Kevin and said, "I can't believe you would do something like this. How long? Hmm? How long have you been–"

Kevin punched her, landing a jab on her chin. Isabel gasped and staggered back, stunned. Kevin hit her again, striking her with a vicious uppercut. Dazed by the blow, Isabel teetered into her doorway.

Upon spotting the blood on her lip, Luke said, "Oh, God. Are you okay? What happened?"

Before he could utter another useless question, Kevin appeared behind his mother. The murderous teenager pushed Isabel into the room, causing his mother to tumble to the floor beside the bed. Disregarding Luke's presence, he entered the room and beat on his mother. He struck down at her with a flurry of punches—jabs, hooks, and uppercuts. He even stomped the back of her head once. He beat her for twenty uninterrupted seconds.

Luke snapped out of his shock and bolted into action. He tackled Kevin. The pair collided with the wall. Luke lowered his head under Kevin's chin and wrapped his arms around the teenager's body. He used a bear hug to try to stop him *without* hitting him.

Eyes burning with rage, Kevin growled as he wiggled in Luke's arms to no avail. He even tried hitting the back of Luke's head with his chin, but the effort was fruitless. So, Kevin leaned forward and pushed back against Luke.

The pair wrestled across the room. They collided with another wall, then they bumped into the nightstand. The lamp fell off of the table and rolled on the floor. The light continued to illuminate the room, though. Banging and grunting sounds echoed through the room as the men grappled in their underwear.

Dazed by the beating, Isabel crawled to the foot of the bed. She turned and gasped as she watched the fight between her lover and her son. *What have I done?*–she thought, blaming herself for the confrontation.

Isabel shouted, "Stop! Please, stop it! Don't do this, boys!"

At that moment, Luke lost his temper. He bellowed, letting out a vicious war cry. He leaned away and grabbed the nape of Kevin's neck, then he thrust the teenager's head into the wall. His head penetrated the drywall, leaving a gaping hole in his wake. Small cuts formed on Kevin's forehead and cheeks. He was dazed by the blow. He staggered away from the wall, then he sat down on the bed.

Luke wasn't going to miss his opportunity to end the fight. He hopped onto the bed and tackled Kevin again. He slid under Kevin's body, then he wrapped his arm around his neck. He held Kevin in a tight rear naked choke-hold. He wasn't trying to strangle him, though.

As he scratched at Luke's forearm, Kevin shouted, "Jacob! Ja... Ja... Jacob, help!"

***

Jacob sat up on his bed and stared at his door. He had heard everything from his bedroom—his mother's shouts, his brother hitting her, and the subsequent fight. His brother's cries for help seeped into his room through the gap under the door. The cries were faint, but he could definitely hear them. *Jacob, help!*—those words haunted him.

"What do I do?" Jacob whispered. "Kevin's the bad guy, isn't he? He started all of this, right? Then, why... why do I want to help him? Why do I still care about him?"

A shrill screeching sound, like heavy furniture scraping a floorboard, echoed through the room. The screeching was accompanied by grunting, croaking, and whimpering sounds.

Jacob sighed, then he reluctantly exited his room. He slowly walked down the hall and approached his mother's bedroom, listening to the sounds of mayhem. The racket grew louder with each step, drilling into his ears. *Kevin could be dying right now,* he thought, *would that be a good or bad thing?*

He stopped in the doorway and gazed into the room. He expected a fight, but he was still surprised. Two men—one young, one old—wrestled in their boxers on his mother's bed. It felt surreal. Luke still held Kevin in the rear naked choke-hold, struggling to keep him under control. Kevin's bloodshot eyes widened with hope upon spotting his brother— Jacob's presence reinvigorated him.

Kevin twisted his body and turned to his left, contorting himself like a possessed girl in a horror movie. He lifted his arm, then he hit Luke's crotch with his elbow. Luke screamed and crossed his legs, weakened by the attack. Kevin fell to his knees beside the bed, coughing and wheezing as he rubbed his neck.

He pointed at Luke and, in a croaky tone, he said, "Jacob... Jacob, *beat him.*"

Tears streaming down her cheeks, Isabel shook her head and cried, "Jacob, baby, get out of here. Go to your room. Don't do this."

"He tried to kill me!" Kevin shouted.

Jacob grimaced and sniffled. The truth dawned onto him: good or evil, killer or friend, he still loved his brother. Family was the most important thing in his life. He didn't agree with his methods, but Kevin *never* abandoned him. So, he couldn't abandon his older brother.

Jacob screamed as he pounced on Luke. He hopped onto the bed and straddled the man's stomach. He pounded Luke's face with the bottom of his clenched fists—*hammerfists.* He practically used his face as a drum. He hit his forehead, his nose, his cheeks, and his mouth. His nose broke with the drubbing. Blood poured out of his nostrils and streamed across his face. Blood oozed from his gums, too, painting his teeth red.

From the foot of the bed, Isabel yelled, "Stop it! Get off of him, Jacob!"

Isabel yelped as Kevin tackled her. The pair landed on the floor between the bed and the dresser.

Isabel said, "Get off of me. Get... Get away from–"

Kevin hit her face with his elbow. The back of her head *thudded* on the floorboard. He hit his mother again, placing all of his weight behind his elbow. Due to his dry, rough skin, the second strike caused a cut to form on her cheek. He didn't stop, though.

He hit her three more times, making sure she was knocked unconscious by the attack.

He whispered, "Go to sleep. I'll take care of you later, okay?"

Kevin breathed heavily as he stood up. He was hurt, exhausted, and frustrated. He glanced over at the bed. Jacob was still hitting their mother's lover, but Luke was putting up a fight. Luke held Jacob's wrists and tried to stop him from beating him.

Kevin grabbed the lamp from the floor, then he jumped onto the bed. He chuckled as he knelt down beside Luke. Violent images flashed in his mind— and that was amusing. He wrapped the lamp's cord around Luke's neck, then he leaned back and tugged on the cord with all of his might. He pulled Luke's head onto his lap, causing Jacob to stumble off of him.

Eyes bulging from his skull, Luke frantically tapped Kevin's arms and grunted, begging for mercy with the gesture. When that didn't work, he moved his hands down and scratched at his own neck. Suffocation was painful and time-consuming. It wasn't like the movies. It took several minutes of *consistent* pressure to strangle someone to death.

Jacob sat on the foot of the bed and watched the strangulation, disgusted. He could see the thick veins on his brother's arms as he tugged on the cord. Kevin's chest and hands reddened due to all of the energy he exerted. Jacob even felt the bed shaking under him as Luke desperately flailed his limbs every which way.

Jacob and Luke stared at each other for a

moment. Jacob's eyes said: *I'm sorry, I don't know what to do.* Luke's eyes, filled with pain and misery, screamed: *help me, don't let me die like this!* They continued to stare at each other throughout the strangulation. One, two, three... *five minutes*—after five long, dreadful minutes, Luke finally passed away.

Luke's legs twitched involuntarily and a gurgling sound emerged from his mouth, but he was dead. There was a hollow look in his eyes.

Absolute certainty was required, though. If he miraculously survived the strangulation, the brothers would surely be imprisoned.

Kevin grabbed a heavy glass ashtray from the nightstand. He screamed as he smashed the ashtray on Luke's forehead. A dull *thudding* sound echoed through the house with each hit. A gash formed over Luke's right eyebrow. Dark blood leaked from the gash and cascaded over his entire face. An indentation, like a giant crater, formed on the right side of his brow. His skull was crushed by the ashtray. The pressure from the attack also caused his eye socket to collapse. Bloody strands of his crushed eye dangled over his cheek.

Jacob couldn't form a single word as he watched the attack. His brother delved deeper into his own depravity with each murder. He felt partly responsible, too. *I let this happen,* he thought, *if I didn't get involved, Luke wouldn't have died.* Once again, guilt burdened his shoulders.

Kevin threw the ashtray aside and said, "*There.* He's dead. He's fucking dead."

He stood up from the bed and stared down at himself. Blood was splattered on his chest, neck, and face. He wiped the blood from his face with the back of his hand, smearing it on his skin.

He muttered, "Stupid bastard... He was stronger than I thought..." He glanced over at Jacob and smiled. He said, "Thanks for the save, little man. I appreciate it. Now I have some other business to handle."

Kevin approached his mother. He rolled Isabel onto her stomach, then he grabbed her ankles and dragged her closer to the door. He pulled her into the light so he could see her better. He lifted her robe, revealing her firm ass. He snickered and licked his lips, then he spanked her. The jiggle of her ass aroused him.

Isabel groaned as she awoke. Weak and bewildered, she turned to her side and glanced down. She couldn't help but cry upon spotting her oldest son standing behind her.

Kevin spanked her again, playfully slapping her other cheek. The erection in his boxers was obvious. Isabel squirmed on the floor, but she could barely move. The room spun around her because of the beating. She could only whimper and wiggle. Like his mother, Jacob knew about his brother's plans: Kevin wanted to rape her. He could see it in his eyes —a glimmer of deviance.

Before Kevin could pull his boxers down, Jacob stood up and shouted, "Don't! You can't do this! Please, Kev, stop it."

Kevin responded, "You can join if you want to

fuck her, too, Jacob. You can finally lose your virginity. If you don't want to fuck her, just leave. I don't want to hear you bitching while I work."

"No, Kev. Stop it, man. We... We can still fix this. We can tell someone. We can, um... We can go see a doctor! They'll help you. Please, don't hurt her—for me."

Kevin gazed into Jacob's eyes. He could see his younger brother was genuine. He sincerely cared about him. He glanced over at his mother, then at his brother, then back at his mother. The decision was obvious to him.

Before Jacob could say another word, Kevin stood up and approached the bed. He punched his brother three times—right, left, *right.* Jacob closed his eyes and fell back on Luke's bloody body. He wrapped his arms around his head and rolled into the fetal position, expecting a brutal barrage of punches to follow. Kevin, however, didn't punch him again.

As he opened his eyes and moved his arms, confused and curious, Jacob saw Kevin standing over him with the bloody ashtray in his hand. His brother smirked—a devilish smile. Kevin struck Jacob's forehead with the ashtray, knocking him unconscious in an instant.

Chapter Eighteen

What Happened?

Jacob opened his eyes to a squint. He breathed deeply through his nose, snorting like a coke addict. He felt the homemade gag in his mouth—a piece of torn fabric that was tightly wrapped around his head. He felt the tight restraints around his wrists, too. His hands were tied to one of the bedposts with the bed sheets.

He opened his eyes a bit more. He rapidly blinked, trying his best to clear his blurred, faded vision. He saw triple, then double.

In a muffled tone, he weakly muttered, "M– Mom... Mom..."

His mother rested her head on the pillow beside him. Her messy hair covered her forehead and cheeks. Her mouth was wide open, blood staining her lips and chin. Due to her wounds, she looked different—as if a completely different person rested on the bed beside him. He recognized her eyes, though. A son could never forget the warmth in his mother's eyes.

There was a problem, though. In spite of his blurred vision, Jacob could see his mother was not blinking. She usually snored when she slept, but her lips didn't flutter and her eyes were open, so he couldn't believe she was sleeping. She wasn't breathing, either. The warmth in her eyes—the love and reassurance—was nothing but a hallucination.

Choking back his tears, the boy mumbled, "I'm... I'm sorry, mom. I'm so sorry. Please, forgive me. Don't... Don't leave me like this. Please, mom, *please*.... Oh, fuck..."

He tightly closed his eyes and whimpered. His vision focused as soon as he opened his eyes again —and he saw a nightmarish sight. His mother's head was decapitated. He had been talking to his mother's severed head all along.

He screamed and cried as he flopped on the bed. His ankles weren't tied, so he kicked every which way. He tried to stand, but his restrained arms stopped him. He stared down at the dresser across from the foot of the bed, then over at the window at the end of the room, then at the ceiling. He glanced at everything, except his mother's head.

"You're awake," Kevin said as he walked into the bedroom.

Jacob glanced over at his brother, terrified. His brother still wore his boxers. He was drenched in blood from head-to-toe, though. As a matter of fact, nearly ninety-percent of his body was painted red with blood. He looked as if he had just climbed out of a pool of red paint.

Kevin chuckled, then he said, "I'm sorry, buddy. I can't believe I forgot that there. It was a mistake. You know I'd never do anything to hurt you."

Jacob winced and trembled as Kevin grabbed their mother's head. He held the decapitated head from a fistful of hair. He approached the dresser, swinging the head back-and-forth as if he were a child capering about with a basket on Easter.

Jacob breathed heavily through his nose as Kevin shoved Isabel's head into a black garbage bag. He still struggled to accept his mother's horrific death. Tears streamed down his rosy cheeks.

There were four other bags in the room and each bag was filled to the brim. Severed arms and legs protruded from the bags. Puddles of blood formed on the floor throughout the entire room. Blood was splattered on the walls and some droplets of blood even managed to land on the ceiling. A sadistic massacre occurred in the bedroom.

Jacob had seen enough horror movies to know exactly what was happening. Despite the shock, he could link the pieces: his brother killed their mother and her boyfriend, and he was working on getting rid of their bodies.

Kevin sat on the edge of the bed beside his brother. He said, "Okay, that's enough of that. No more games. I'm going to take the gag out of your mouth, okay? But, if you scream... *If* you scream, I'm going to cut your tongue off, then I'll chop your body up and get rid of you just like mom. You understand me?"

Unadulterated fear glimmered in Jacob's eyes. He panted and trembled uncontrollably. Mucus dripped from his nose, tears gushed from his eyes. Of course, he couldn't just say 'no.' His brother just killed their mother, so he was sure he would be willing to kill him, too.

His bottom lip quivering, Jacob nodded—*okay.* Kevin slipped his bloody fingers under the homemade gag, smearing blood on Jacob's cheek. He tugged on the torn fabric until he pulled the gag over Jacob's bottom lip. Jacob gasped for air and lifted his head from the pillow. The siblings stared at each other for a moment—a short, awkward minute.

His voice cracking, Jacob stuttered, "Wha–What happened? What did... Fuck, man, what did you do?"

Kevin responded, "It's obvious, isn't it? They're dead, Jacob."

"Wh–Why? Huh? Why... Why did you kill them? Why did you kill her? She was our... She was *my* mom... She loved us! Why did you do it?"

"Oh, you want the *full* story. Well, while you were sleeping, I went back and fucked her. Yeah, I fucked our mom. I even cummed inside of her. She cried, but... she accepted it. I think she even liked it. But, I wasn't done. I pushed her cheeks aside, then I fucked her ass. She didn't like that, though, so she put up a fight. One thing led to another and I ended up killing her. I choked that bitch to death. I wish I didn't have to do that, but she didn't give me a choice."

Did you give her a choice?—Jacob wanted to blurt out the question, but he couldn't utter a word. His brother confessed to raping and killing their mother —and he didn't show a shred of remorse.

Kevin said, "I already cut up their bodies in the bathroom so we're almost done. I mean, you were knocked out for a *long* time, Jacob. Well, maybe you weren't knocked out. Maybe you were actually sleeping. You haven't been getting a lot of sleep lately, have you?"

A normal conversation—Jacob was amazed. His brother committed a double-homicide, the siblings were surrounded by carnage, but Kevin still wanted to have a normal conversation. The entire situation was nightmarish. He could barely imagine their bizarre conversation. *Hey, I just killed our mom and her boyfriend. Crazy weather we're having, huh?*

Kevin chuckled, then he said, "Anyway, we have something important to talk about."

"What?"

"Our options. Well, they're more like *your* options since you'll be making the final decision. So, here's what we can do: we can hide the bodies and tell the police our mom ran off with Luke. This option is good because it lets us stay together. You see, I'm turning eighteen in a few weeks. When that happens, I think I'll be able to adopt you, Jacob. We can live happily ever after, little man."

The first option would have been delightful weeks ago. After all, at that moment, he loved his brother and he hated his own life. Due to Jacob's recent epiphany, though, he couldn't easily make the decision. He didn't want to be associated with the killer anymore.

Jacob stuttered, "Wha–What are the... the other options?"

"Well, if you don't want to live in this place—and I understand if you don't—we can always run away and live as hobos. We can set-up a little shanty in the No-Light District. People will respect us there and we can have a lot of fun. The final option... The final option isn't great for you, little man. If you want, I can kill you before you snitch and I can live the bachelor lifestyle. I've always wanted a place of my own. So... what will it be?"

Jacob stared at his brother with a steady expression, then he grimaced and cried. All of the options were horrible. He couldn't live with a guilty conscience, he disliked the No-Light District because of their past actions, and he definitely didn't want his brother to kill him. Unless they were suicidal, people hardly ever willfully welcomed death.

Kevin snickered and caressed Jacob's cheek. He said, "Don't cry, Jacob. Listen, if you want my opinion, I prefer the first two options because then I won't have to kill you. I know things are scary right now, I know what I did to mom, but I don't want to hurt *you.* I love you, and that's coming from my heart."

Jacob responded, "I... I don't know if I can keep your secret, Kev. You... You went too far. You ki-killed my–" A lump of anxiety formed in his throat while he was speaking. He loudly swallowed, then he said, "You killed my mom. I... I loved her so much. My–My brain won't let me keep that secret. It's too much."

"You don't really have a choice. If you somehow managed to tell anyone about this later, you'd still be in trouble. Your hands are dirty. You may not have killed anyone, but you helped me every step of the way. Shit, man, I could even blame everything on you. I'm a fuckin' pro at this, Jacob. You? You're an amateur. You probably left more DNA at every crime scene than I did. Think about that before you make your choice."

Jacob wheezed and groaned. He looked away from his brother as he cried. A mishmash of emotions swelled in his timid body—shame, sadness, fear, *anger.*

Without glancing over at his brother, he said, "The first one. We–We'll get rid of 'em, then... then we'll stay together."

"Good choice, good choice," Kevin responded. As he untied Jacob's wrists, Kevin said, "Like I said, I've already done most of the dirty work. So, we only have to get rid of the bodies."

"H–How?"

"I really wanted to melt them in the bathtub, but I don't have all of the stuff for that. So, we're going to bury them in the backyard before sunrise. I need you to get the shovel from the storage closet and start digging a hole outside—a *big* hole. I'll drag these bags out so we can bury their limbs first, then we'll move the torsos out of the bathroom. They're heavy as fuck, though, so we'll need to work together to get rid of them. After we finish that, we'll clean up the place, fix up the backyard, and all of that shit... then we're done."

Jacob furrowed his brow and asked, "Is that it? It's... It's that simple?"

"It's that simple," Kevin responded. He patted Jacob's shoulder and said, "We'll get our stories straight later, then we'll call the cops in the afternoon. Come on, let's get started."

Chapter Nineteen

I Love You

Jacob shambled out of the bedroom, his legs trembling with each step. He felt lightheaded, disoriented, and nauseous. In the hallway, he bumped into the wall to his left, then he crashed into the wall to his right. Leaning on the wall, he closed his eyes and took a deep breath. *Keep moving,* he thought, *don't stop until it's over.*

He took another deep breath, then he stared into the room to his left—*the bathroom.* The light was on in the room so he could see everything. The floor and the walls were splattered with blood. Two bloodied torsos—limbless and headless—floated in a bathtub full of blood. One of the torsos belonged to his mother.

Death stained the bathroom with acrid air, carrying the pungent scent of blood throughout the house. With the savage murders, the home became a slaughterhouse for humans.

Teary-eyed, Jacob pinched his nose and whispered, "I'm sorry, mom. I'm... I'm so sorry."

He walked down the hall and opened the last door to his left. He ran his eyes over the tools in the closet. The storage closet was used to store supplies for the backyard as well as general home improvement products, but most of the tools had not been used in years. Dust and cobwebs clung to everything in the closet. A few spiders even skittered across the walls.

Jacob grabbed the shovel. He stopped before he could close the door. The hand cultivator called his name. He remembered helping his mother in the garden when he was a small child, breaking up the soil with the cultivator—that was before her sex addiction. The memory wasn't significant, though. Instead, he thought about beating his brother to death with the cultivator.

I could do it, he thought, *and he wouldn't see it coming.* At heart, he knew his brother would be able to overpower him at the first sign of trouble. He was weak, mentally and physically.

Jacob walked out to the center of the backyard. He thrust the shovel into the grass and started digging. Sweat streamed down his brow and veins bulged on his forearms. A warm sensation spread across his trembling arms. Dirt stained his flannel pajamas and bare feet. The sound of digging echoed through the cul-de-sac, but their neighbors didn't seem to care.

Two hours passed at a snail's pace.

Jacob stood in the hole. He stared down at his grubby feet, disappointed. The hole was three feet wide, four feet long, and three feet deep. Kevin walked out the back door with the last bag of severed limbs. He sat the bag beside the four other bags near the grill, then he approached the hole.

He rubbed his hands together and said, "It's not deep enough. You want to make sure they're buried *real* deep, Jacob. You don't want a dog to dig 'em up."

"I'm tired," Jacob responded, still avoiding eye contact. "I... I need a break."

"Yeah, sure. I'm done gutting the bodies anyway. Give me the shovel. Let me do it."

Kevin jumped into the hole. He took the shovel and started digging. Jacob climbed out of the ditch. He stood near the ditch and watched his brother, surprised. He thought: *how can he act like nothing happened? Didn't he love her?*

Between breaths, as he dug, Kevin said, "This is... going to be great. We can finally... live free. She can't tell us what to do... The government can't tell us what to do, either. We'll bring girls back to our bachelor pad... and we'll fuck them all. We can even keep mom's head. You can, you know, use her for practice."

Jacob heard enough from his brother. He walked away from the hole, ignoring Kevin's disgusting chatter. He dug his fingers into his hair and walked in circles around the tree. He felt like kicking and screaming, but he knew he would be killed for such a foolish outburst.

He stopped in his tracks upon spotting a shiny object in the dirt near the tree. Like the hand cultivator in the closet, the object called to him. He leaned forward with his hands on his knees, trying to get a better view of the item. His jaw dangled in amazement. He found himself staring at Wyatt's switchblade—the same blade the bully used to threaten him during his birthday party.

He grabbed the knife and whispered, "I can still stop him..."

He turned around and stared up at the sky. The cul-de-sac was still dominated by darkness, but the sun was beginning to rise beyond the horizon.

"Hey!" Kevin shouted from the ditch. Jacob glanced over at his brother. Kevin said, "I think that's a long enough break. Listen, if we work together, we can finish this in thirty minutes. Come on, you can use your hands or something."

"O–Okay..."

Jacob hid the switchblade by cupping his hand. He walked towards the ditch, trying his best to act natural. Yet, with each step forward, the distance between him and the hole appeared to grow larger. He felt as if he were walking through a dream. His brother didn't notice, though. He continued digging as he babbled about their plans.

Jacob slid into the ditch. He stood face-to-face with his brother. He watched as his lips flapped, but he didn't hear a word. *I can't keep living like this,* he thought, *I have to kill him to stop myself from killing.*

Jacob pressed the button on the switchblade, causing a *snapping* sound to emerge in the backyard. Kevin stopped digging—he recognized the sound.

Before a word could be uttered, Jacob thrust the blade into Kevin's stomach. Kevin staggered and screamed in pain. He leaned on the side of the ditch as he stared down at his abs. Blood leaked from the stab wound above his belly button.

Jacob screamed as he stabbed him again. He thrust the blade directly *through* his belly button. He pulled the blade out, then he stabbed him once again. The blade penetrated the area under his belly button.

Kevin grabbed Jacob's wrist. Out of breath, he stammered, "S–Stop... Pl–Please, s–stop..."

Jacob pulled away from his brother's grip. He quickly stabbed him two more times—once in the lower abdomen, the other in his upper abdomen. If it weren't for his ribs, the blade would have penetrated his stomach again.

Kevin hissed with each stab. He cried and wheezed, debilitated by the insufferable pain. Jacob could see the truth in his brother's eyes. Kevin was afraid of death. He was a monster, but he was also human.

Kevin barked, "*Stop!*" He clambered out of the ditch, then he crawled to the side of the house. He yelled, "Help! He... He's trying to kill me! Fuck, he's gone crazy!"

Jacob followed his brother to the side of the house. He repeatedly thrust the blade into Kevin's lower back as they squeezed past the old patio furniture. *Nine, ten times?*—he lost count of how many times he stabbed his own brother, but that didn't stop him from thrusting the blade into Kevin's shoulder.

The brothers burst through the gate on the side of the house. They tumbled on the lawn, surrounded by overgrown grass and trash.

Kevin slid out from under his brother. Dazed by the loss of blood, he stumbled through the front gate and crashed into his mother's car. Jacob glanced around the cul-de-sac, awed. Nosy neighbors watched the commotion from their windows, porches, and cars. Some of the neighbors retreated to their homes upon spotting the blood.

Determined, Jacob marched forward and sternly said, "You have to die. *Now.*"

Blood and saliva dripping from his mouth, Kevin cried, "Wha–What the fuck, little man? Why are you doing this? I was... I was going to let you live. I loved you! I fucking loved you, Jacob!"

Kevin fell to the ground towards the center of the circular end of the cul-de-sac. Jacob straddled his brother's waist, then he stabbed down at his chest. Blood spewed from the stab wounds like lava from a volcano. Due to his severe loss of blood, Kevin couldn't muster the energy to fight or shout. Jacob refused to spare his brother during his fit of rage anyway.

"Jacob!" a feminine voice echoed through the cul-de-sac.

Jacob stopped. He held the knife over his head, blood dripping from the tip of the blade. He recognized the voice. He glanced up and stared at the house to his right. As expected, Molly stood near her front gate, a blanket draped over her shoulders. The young girl wrestled with her father on the front lawn, trying her best to reach Jacob, but to no avail. Her mother watched from the porch, blatantly frightened.

Molly grabbed the chain-link fence and cried, "Jacob! Please, don't do it! It's okay to be good! You can... You can be different! Don't hurt him anymore! Stop it!"

Teary-eyed, the brothers turned towards each other. In each other's eyes, they could see reflections of themselves.

Breathing erratically, Kevin weakly said, "I'm... I'm... I'm sorry, little man. I fucked up. I... I just couldn't control myself. I... I didn't lie, though. I wanted us to work together because... because I loved you. I was so lonely, man, and... and I knew you were, too. I thought it would work out. I'm sorry..."

Jacob's tears plopped on Kevin's cheeks. He could sense the sincerity behind his brother's words. He could finally feel his remorse, he could finally read his heart. *I killed the monster,* he thought, *and I killed my brother, too.*

Jacob said, "I'm sorry. I didn't know what else to do. You killed her... You killed *them.* I had to stop you, but that doesn't mean I didn't love you. I... I love you, too, Kev."

Kevin blankly stared up at the sky. His chest didn't rise, his lips didn't flutter. Jacob recognized the hollow look in his eyes—the look of death. He could only wonder if his brother heard his apology before he passed away.

Jacob staggered to his feet, the knife clenched in his right hand. He dug his fingers into his hair and glanced around the neighborhood. All eyes were on him.

Wailing police sirens disrupted the already hectic morning. A black-and-white police cruiser sped towards the end of the cul-de-sac. The vehicle swerved left-and-right, then it skidded to a stop ten meters away from the siblings. A middle-aged police officer with grizzled hair climbed out of the car. He stood behind his door and drew his handgun.

Aiming at Jacob, the officer shouted, "Put the weapon down! Put it down!"

At that moment, images of death flooded Jacob's mind. He thought about Dean, the homeless man, Wyatt, his mother, and Luke. He didn't kill any of them, but, one way or another, all of the deaths would be linked to him. He towered over his brother's body with a bloody knife in his hand. He would rightfully be blamed for Kevin's murder, at least.

Prison or death—those were his only options. If he had to die, he figured he'd let the cop kill him. It seemed simple enough. He lifted the knife up to his shoulder, the blade pointing at the cop. He took a step forward. He could hear Molly crying from her lawn, but he was determined to die at the hands of the police officer—*suicide by cop.*

The officer muttered, "Shit..." As he stepped in reverse, he holstered his firearm, then he drew his taser from his belt. He aimed at Jacob and said, "I know what you're doing, kid. I'm not going to shoot you, I'm not going to kill you. It doesn't have to end like that. Just put the weapon down, okay? Put it down and talk to me."

Jacob was shocked. Due to the media's fear-mongering, he believed most cops were trigger-happy. The officer showed restraint and compassion, though. The officer and the child reached an impasse: the officer's taser couldn't hit

Jacob from afar and Jacob couldn't reach the officer without getting tasered.

If you cut his jugulars, he'll die in a few minutes — Kevin's advice echoed through Jacob's mind. It was perfect. Teary-eyed, the teenager glanced over at Molly and mouthed: *thank you.*

Before anyone could stop him, Jacob thrust the blade into his own neck. He severed his jugular. Tears streamed across his cheeks as he grimaced in pain. He pulled the knife out, then he quickly stabbed himself again. He felt the blood clogging his throat and coursing down his chest. The knife fell to the floor and Jacob fell to his knees. He trembled with fear, his teeth chattering and eyelids flickering.

As she was dragged back into her house, Molly cried, "Jacob! No!"

The officer holstered his taser and muttered, "Damn it..."

The cop sprinted to Jacob's side. He knelt down beside the boy and placed pressure on his wounds. He glanced over at Kevin—he was long gone. He could only save one of them. He grunted as he lifted Jacob from the ground. He carried him back to his car, one arm under his legs and the other supporting his back. He laid him on his side in the backseat of his car.

He ran to the trunk of the cruiser and riffled through his first-aid kit. He pulled a gauze roll out of the kit, he closed the trunk, then he rushed back to Jacob. He sloppily wrapped the roll around his neck, then he placed Jacob's hands over his own wounds. He knew he couldn't stop the bleeding with his first-aid kit, so his priority was getting him to a hospital.

The officer said, "It's going to be okay, kid. Hold your neck, okay? Put some pressure on that and you'll... you'll be fine. I'm going to get you to a hospital."

The officer slammed the door, then he climbed into the driver's seat. The wheels howled as he sped off. Over the wailing sirens, he reported the incident, he described Kevin's death, and he announced Jacob's imminent arrival at the nearest hospital.

Jacob cracked a smile as he stared at the ceiling of the car. Although the ride was bumpy, he felt as if he were being cradled in his mother's arms. He didn't hear the officer's voice, either. Instead, he heard Kevin's voice. His family was calling to him, inviting him to the afterlife. He couldn't resist the call. He wanted to feel his mother's embrace again, he wanted to speak to his brother one more time. He pulled the gauze away from his wounds and allowed himself to bleed out.

In a raspy tone, he whispered, "I'm... coming... home."

The pain dwindled and a frightening numbness set in. His vision faded, growing darker with each passing second. His heart slowed, too. He closed his eyes and accepted death. With a smile on his face, he passed away in the back seat of the police cruiser.

Join the mailing list!

There are rotten apples in *every* family. Want to meet more deviant families? Are you craving more *extreme* horror? If so, I have great news: I release new horror books *every* month. In fact, I actually release a new book every 28 days, so that's thirteen books per year. If you sign-up for my mailing list, I'll let you know about every new release. You'll also receive updates about book deals, free books, and the occasional giveaway. Best of all, it requires very little effort on your part and it's completely free! Oh, and you'll only receive 1-2 emails per month—no spam, I promise. Click here to sign-up: http://eepurl.com/bNl1CP

Dear Reader,

Hey! First and foremost, thanks for reading *Rotten Apples.* This was a disturbing book to write, so I'm guessing it was a disturbing book to read. From its troubled characters to its graphic descriptions of murder, this might be my most disturbing book to date. It's definitely up there with *The Abuse of Ashley Collins* and *Mason's Television.* As usual, there were warnings plastered all over the book and on the product page. If you accidentally wandered into this book and if it truly disturbed you, please accept my sincerest apologies. I want to shed light on true human horror, but I never plan on offending anyone with my writing.

Usually, my books are inspired by classic novels, horror movies, or real crimes. *Rotten Apples* wasn't really inspired by anything *specific,* though. I suppose my main inspiration was my general interest in child killers. Since I was a Criminal Justice student in college, I've always been interested in criminology—the mind of a criminal, specifically. I've spent quite a bit of time studying serial killers and child killers. I think children who kill are terrifying. To be able to kill at such a young age—without truly understanding one's own actions—shows a sort of *primal* personality. I don't know if I explained that right, but I think you know what I mean.

While writing this book, I also wanted to go back

to my roots. My most popular novel is *A Family of Violence.* If you're a fan of my books, that's probably the novel that introduced you to my work. So, with *Rotten Apples,* I wanted to create a spiritual successor to *A Family of Violence.* I've had readers ask about a sequel to *A Family of Violence* and that obviously hasn't happened, so I hope this quenches your thirst for books about troubled children and families. I really tried to match the themes, the atmosphere, and the pacing with this one. What did you think? Is it a worthy successor?

Anyway, if you enjoyed this book, *please* leave a review on Amazon.com. Your reviews help me improve on my writing and I also gain exposure on Amazon. With that, I can write better books while gaining more readers. With more readers, I can publish more books. Sounds great, doesn't it? So, *please* leave a review.

Writing a review doesn't have to take your whole afternoon, either. You can write a review in a matter of minutes. Detailed reviews really help, but sometimes you just don't have a lot to say. I get it. So, here are a few questions to help you. Did you like the story? Was this book too violent, was it not violent enough for an extreme horror novel, or was it just right? Do you like these realistic, disturbing horror stories? Or do you prefer my funner, violent slashers? Answering questions like these will help me understand you, the reader. Your words have the power to influence my writing—please use them wisely.

Want to show more support? Share this book with your friends and family on all of your favorite social media websites. Put up a link on Twitter and Facebook. Share a picture on Instagram or Snapchat. Tell your friends about it on Skype. Have a pen pal in a different country? Hell, have a pen pal in prison? Send them a paperback! Share a book—*any book*—with the world! Remember, word-of-mouth is a great way to support independent authors—and it's mostly *free*.

This is where I usually update you on my financial situation to guilt you into reading more of my books. (No, that's not really the reason. I'm just trying to be funny.) I still don't have much of an update. Your support is helping me live a pretty humble life. I promise, though: if I ever get rich, you will be the first to know. I like to be transparent.

Finally, if you're a horror fan, feel free to visit my Amazon's Author page. I've published *eighteen* horror novels, a few sci-fi/fantasy books, and some anthologies. Want to read a violent slasher? Check out *Cannibal Creek*. Looking for a *Texas Chainsaw Massacre*-style novel? Check out my next book, *Spit and Die.* Keep your eyes open for my upcoming novels since I release a new book every month. Feel free to check out my older novels in the meantime, too. It helps and I really appreciate it! Once again, thank you for reading. Your readership keeps me going through the darkest times!

Until our next venture into the dark and disturbing,
Jon Athan

P.S. If you have questions (or insults), you can contact me via Twitter @Jonny_Athan, or my Facebook page, or through my business email: info@jon-athan.com. If you're an aspiring author, I'm always happy to offer a helping hand. Even if you only have a simple question, don't hesitate to contact me. Thanks again!